*My Chaos Theory*

ALSO BY STEVE WATKINS

*The Black O: Racism and Redemption*
*in an American Corporate Empire*

# MY
# CHAOS
# THEORY

*Stories*

Steve Watkins

SOUTHERN METHODIST
UNIVERSITY PRESS

Requests for permission to reproduce material from this work should be sent to:
Rights and Permissions
Southern Methodist University Press
PO Box 750415
Dallas, Texas 75275-0415

Grateful acknowledgment is made to the editors of the publications in which the following stories first appeared:

*Apalachee Quarterly*: "My Chaos Theory"
*Apalachee Review*: "Bocky Bocky"
*Denver Quarterly*: "Ice Age"
*Greensboro Review*: "Driver's Ed"
*Mississippi Review*: "Critterworld" (also published in *The Pushcart Prize Anthology* and *100 Percent Pure Florida Fiction*) and "Camouflage"
*North American Review*: "Desgraciado"
*Quarterly West*: "Adam's House"
*Sequoia*: "A Jelly of Light"
*Snake Nation Review*: "Painting the Baby's Room" and "Kafka's Sister"
*washington review*: "Family of Man"

Cover photograph © 2003 Scott Allan Wallick, www.plaintxt.org
Jacket and text design: Tom Dawson

Library of Congress Cataloging-in-Publication Data
Watkins, Steve, 1954–
    My chaos theory : stories / by Steve Watkins. — 1st ed.
       p. cm.
    Twelve stories about the secret ways of men and boys dealing with things in life.
    Contents: Critterworld — Bocky-Bocky — Family of man — Desgraciado — A jelly of light — Painting the baby's room — Kafka's sister — Adam's house — Ice Age — Driver's ed — Camouflage — My chaos theory.
    ISBN-13: 978-0-87074-512-6 (acid-free paper)
    ISBN-10: 0-87074-512-3 (acid-free paper)
     I. Title.

PS3623.A86945M9 2006
813'.6—dc22

2006044384

Printed in the United States of America on acid-free paper

10  9  8  7  6  5  4  3  2  1

*For Janet*

# Acknowledgments

I could not have written the stories in this book without the help and inspiration of many wonderful people, none more than my friends Bucky McMahon and Pamela Ball, my wife Janet Marshall Watkins, and my friend and teacher, the late Jerome Stern, who I still miss every day. I can't imagine a better editor than Kathryn Lang at SMU Press, and I'm not the first to say so; her admirers are legion, and I am grateful for the opportunity to have become one of them. Many thanks also to George Ann Ratchford and Keith Gregory at SMU. Jesse Kercheval, Janet Burroway, Mary Jane Ryals, Laura Newton, Joe Straub, Lauren Lustig, David Williams, Wayne, Clyde, and Norie Watkins, Johanna Branch, Helen Felsing, Steve Farmer, Rowland Folensbee, John Hudson, Neva Trenis, Patrick Neustatter, the real John and George, and my grandmother, who we called Viva—all have taught me plenty, and I thank them plenty. I especially thank my daughters Maggie, Eva, Claire, and Lili. It's a blessing to get to be their dad.

# Contents

# Critterworld

First the rumors.

No, Henry's Meats didn't come around with their knives to carve steaks from the body. Mutt & Jeff's Grill didn't serve elephant-burgers.

Nobody sawed off the feet for umbrella stands. Nobody caught any weird African diseases, no elephantiasis. The little girl from Michigan, the one who got trapped in the car, she might have seen a psychiatrist for a while, but if she did it was back up North, so I don't see how anybody could have known for sure about that story, true or not.

And the elephant's name wasn't Stash, like "trash." It was Stash, like in "lost."

But people will say anything, I know that now, especially in a little town like ours, and I guess the best thing is not to even listen, though I don't see how that's possible unless you go deaf. You could still do everything you wanted if you were deaf. You could even make great music, like Beethoven; you just wouldn't be able to hear it is all.

I told my mother that after what happened to Stash. My mother was the only one I talked to for a long time, maybe about a month. But she just hugged me and said, "Oh Charlie, do you know what? That Beethoven story is so sad it always makes me cry."

We were there when it happened, of course—me and Jun Morse and George Mabry—out by 301 a mile south of town, sitting in the ditch across the road, pretty well hidden behind the tall weeds and under the billboard that said CRITTERWORLD, FLORIDA'S FIRST ZOO, which I always thought was kind of a lie, because it made you think *first ever* when it was really just the first you got to when you crossed the state line. Jun and George were doing their Advanced Geometry homework. We were all three in the accelerated class. In fact, we *were* the accelerated class. They drove us over to high school from eighth grade so we could sit in a room full of eleventh graders who tried to cheat off our tests. I liked it more than Jun and George, though, because I shared my book with this one girl named Sharla, who was a cheerleader but still pretty nice, and she would scoot her desk right next to mine, and sometimes when we were both hunched over the book my elbow touched her boob, but she didn't move and either didn't know or didn't mind, and I kept it there as long as I could until I lost all the feeling in my arm.

Anyway, the other guys were doing geometry, and I was watching Stash when it happened. One minute he was standing there, this hundred-year-old elephant, not moving except for the ends of his big flappy ears, and it might have been a breeze doing that. The next minute he seemed to sort of wobble. He lifted his chained leg, looked at it as if he'd just realized what they'd done to him, even though he'd been chained to that iron ring in front of Critterworld for as long as anybody could remember. He raised his trunk. He swung his head from side to side, made a noise that sounded like all the air rushing from his body, then fell sideways on top of the Volkswagen.

I stood straight up and stepped on George's homework. All I could think about at first was why did they park their car so close to Stash? The explanation later, the one the father of the little girl gave to the Jacksonville paper, was they didn't think Stash was alive. Stash was so still, and so dusty from standing there all those years by the highway, that they thought he was a statue of an elephant, like over in Weeki Wachee they have that brontosaurus that's really a gas station, or like out West my mother told me about a World's Biggest Prairie Dog.

Since there's nothing once you get south of town except scrub brush, slash pine, and Critterworld, and since the little girl's parents were inside the Critterworld snack shop, I was the first to hear her screaming inside the car. And initially I didn't believe it was somebody screaming, because Stash flattened the car so badly that I couldn't see how there could be anybody inside. George was yelling at me to get off his geometry homework, too, so that made it hard to hear anything else. George is just anal about his homework anyway—writes everything out on graph paper in this tiny block print that looks like a computer wrote it, which you might say is sort of the case, because when they did the eighth grade aptitude test it was old George Mabry that not only scored in the 99th percentile but actually answered all the questions and didn't miss one. They announced it at an assembly. Jun and I and two girls were in the 90th percentile, but Jun—whose real name used to be John until he decided he needed to change it—told me all the tests really measured was your ability to take tests. Somehow to him that meant that being in the 90th or even the 99th percentile was, to use his favorite phrase, a meaningless abstraction, but I didn't see how it was meaningless, since my whole life seemed to be about taking tests, so it was comforting to know I was good at it. When you make all A's, you just figure they're grading on the curve, and most of the kids in class aren't too smart, so your A is a relative thing, to use another one of Jun's favorite phrases. But when they rank you with the whole state of Florida, you have to figure there are some pretty smart people out there that you're up against.

Not that I ever felt as smart as Jun or George. Even though everybody lumped us together as the eggheads of junior high and all because of our grades and because we hung out together and because we played chess in homeroom, I always thought I was pulling something over on the teachers, working really, really hard to seem like I was as smart as them, when the truth was that I'm not actually all that intelligent. I said that to my mother after the time I got accused of cheating on a science test. A kid had told the teacher I looked on George's answer sheet, when all I was really doing was seeing how far along George was on the test, which of course was a lot further along than me. Nothing happened, though, because Mrs. Crow said she knew I would never cheat, and besides, what was that kid doing looking around during a test anyway? Still, I was pretty upset, and I told my mother I thought I was getting an ulcer from trying to pretend I was as smart as George and Jun.

What she said was, "Of course you're smart, Charlie. Just maybe not in the same way as your friends. You have an intuitive intelligence."

The funny thing was that nobody really cared if I was smart, or if Jun was, or if George was. I mean, teachers cared, and our parents cared, and George and Jun certainly cared about themselves. George already had a correspondence going with the registrar at M.I.T., and I'm not making that up. But other kids didn't care, and I only cared in a weird way, because being smart, or pretending to be smart, was about the only thing I was good at. It was all I had. I couldn't play basketball, even though I worked at it all the time. I wasn't big enough or fast enough or strong enough. I didn't know how to talk to girls, except for smart girls about school subjects, and except for that cheerleader, Sharla, who talked to me sometimes about things, like the difference between dancing and dance. Dancing was what she loved to do; dance was what she wanted to study when she got to college. But she had a football-player boyfriend, and whenever she was with him I pretty much ceased to exist.

But there I was, anyway—to get back to the story—standing on George Mabry's graph paper, staring across the road, shaking my head to figure out if that really was somebody screaming. It was Jun who made the first move. He stood beside me and said, "Stash! Wow!" and then he said, "Squashed bug!" He grabbed my arm and we both ran across the highway to the car. George was too busy collecting his papers and books to come right away.

We could just see the little girl's face through what was left of the passenger door window; Stash had pretty much flattened the driver's side. The girl was flat on the floor of the car, screaming in a way that sounded more like squealing—like *Hreeeee-hreeeee-hreeeee*—and I think it was as much to get her to stop as anything else that I started pushing like crazy against Stash to get him off the car. That's how stupid I was.

Jun ran inside Critterworld to get help. He told me later that when he came back out with the parents I was hitting Stash's head with my fists and yelling at him to get up, but that's not how I remember it. I just remember pushing and pushing, and dust rising off Stash in little puffs right in my face, and not really figuring out he was dead until the girl's father shoved me out of the way and I stepped back and looked into one of those big elephant eyes that was wide open but already dusted over too.

A dozen cars stopped, some of them right there in the highway, before the sheriffs finally showed up. The little girl had quit squealing by then—partly because she'd figured out she wasn't going to die, and partly because Jun got her a bottle of Coke from Critterworld and stuck about ten straws together into one long one to reach her mouth. The father yelled at Jun when he first brought it out, but the mother said, "Let the boy help, Clyde," and the father got a little nicer after that, and they threaded the straw through a crack in what was left of the window and down to the girl trapped on the floor.

After that, Jun moved off a short ways from the crowd. He couldn't stand crowds. He told me once that he was an *ascetic*, and that there were two kinds: the ones that choose it, as a means to something, and the ones that are born to it, the ones like him. That was supposed to explain his aversion to crowds. At the time I didn't even know what he meant by *ascetic*, and when I looked it up I had the wrong spelling so I went around for a long time with the wrong definition in my head. I did the same thing with *cavalry* and *Calvary*, too, but that was in second grade.

I didn't want to leave Stash when Jun moved away. Everybody was so mad at him for dying and crushing the VW and trapping the little Michigan girl, I guess I felt like Stash needed somebody on his side, an advocate or something, even though he was dead. Not that I said anything to anybody. I laid my hand on the bottom of his foot, which was crusty because it was so old, but still not hard like you might expect, and I tried to remember everything I had read about elephants. The only line that came to me, though, was this one: "The powerful feet can trample an attacker into the ground but are so softly cushioned that a whole herd of elephants can troop through a forest without making a sound."

George Mabry, meanwhile, wasn't having any problems remembering. He was over in front of the monkey cage where they kept the psycho-monkey that everybody flicked cigarette butts at, and he was lecturing some kids about elephant penises. For such a math-and-science nut, it's amazing how much George Mabry went in for the dirty stuff. He told those kids that an elephant penis weighs sixty pounds, and it gets four feet long when the elephant gets aroused, and sometimes, if the elephant is chasing a cow, he might even step on it. And he told them about how the penis is shaped sort of like an S, and the muscles at the end work on their own to poke around under the cow's belly to find the hole, which is way up underneath, not right there between the hind legs.

For some reason it really bothered me that George was telling them all that. I knew it, too, of course—Jun had given both of us the same book to read—but George was just showing off how much he knew and what a dirty mind he had. Those kids, though, they didn't deserve to know that stuff. They hadn't earned the right like we had. It didn't seem appropriate, or fair, or something, that they should get it so cheaply, and for a minute I hated George Mabry, standing there in his high-water pants and nerd glasses with that hair he never washed, trying to be cool with those elementary school kids, trying to be cool like I knew none of us would ever be cool, not him or me or even Jun, who always knew what to say and never had to show it off like George, the M.I.T. nerd.

I saw all of us in that second as these three very brainy but mostly very pathetic guys who didn't have any friends but one another, and even those friendships as a sort of last resort because nobody else would have us. I looked at Stash's old yellow tusks, or what was left of them since they'd been sawed off short before I ever knew him, and I looked down between his legs and saw just this shriveled worm of a penis, and I felt like crying and I felt like everything that had happened was my fault, as dumb as that may sound, but it was how I felt and in some ways how I still feel, no matter what my mother said later to cheer me up and no matter what sometimes I can think of to tell myself.

The girl was still trapped in the car, and the sheriffs, as it turned out, didn't have a clue for getting her free, and that's the way things stood for a while, except for one thing I haven't mentioned yet, which is why Jun and George and I happened to be there in the first place, hiding out in the ditch across the highway from Critter-world. It was because we were studying old Stash and looking for a way to kill him ourselves.

Critterworld is the saddest place in Florida, maybe even in America. I only went inside once, and that was on a field trip in elementary school. Stash out front was so familiar to us that we hardly noticed him—all except Jun, who made a point of saying how much Stash disgusted him—and the psycho-monkey in the cage was already mean way back then from picking up lit cigarettes. When people came near he attacked the bars and tried to throw things, but for some reason he couldn't stop himself from picking up cigarette butts and burning his hands. All us kids crowded around the cage and teased him with monkey noises that day of the field trip, which frustrated him and made him crash wildly around, hurling himself at the bars as if he wanted to kill us or kill himself trying.

Pay a dollar and you could go inside where they had the two-headed turtle collection, and the Siamese piglets disintegrating in a giant jar of formaldehyde. The whole place smelled of formalde-hyde, as a matter of fact—that and the vomity smell of very old, very wet straw. There were the snakes, of course, and all the girls cried when they saw the white rat shivering in a corner of the aquarium where they kept the boa constrictor. And there was the bald eagle with the broken wing that hadn't healed right so it couldn't fly. And the albino squirrels, and the furry chinchillas, and the Shetland pony. In the petting area they kept a lamb and a goat and a calf and a live piglet and a goose, but Jun told me Critterworld sold them all for slaughter except the goose once they grew past the cute-baby stage. Nobody liked the goose because he bit kids.

Our first plan—or rather Jun's first plan—was to get rid of all of Critterworld, maybe burn it down, but we quickly dropped that because it was too ambitious. "And besides," Jun told us, "the point is not to draw attention to ourselves or to the deed."

"Then what is the point?" I asked him—this was in homeroom a couple of weeks before everything happened, and Jun and George were playing chess while we debated our course of action.

George put Jun in check just then, and Jun glared at me as if it was my fault but also as if to say, "We can't keep going over and over this for you, Charlie." He was mad at me for bringing it up again, but I was still having a hard time figuring out why it meant so much to Jun to kill something. I mean, I understood the reasons he *said*, but Jun seemed so obsessive. That was the word my mother used for it later, anyway, and she said she thought it had something to do with Jun's father, who used to be head of maintenance at the hospital but lost a lot of jobs because of drinking and now ran a service station north of town out by the interstate. That made a lot of sense in a Sigmund Freud kind of way, I guess, but somehow when you're in the middle of things it all seems a lot more complicated, and with Jun, who could talk me into just about anything if he talked long enough, I'm still not sure.

The point, as he had explained a hundred times, was to kill a thing that had compromised itself so much that it no longer had a self. Something that wasn't true to its nature. Jun started talking about "essence" like it was something you could put in your book bag or hide in your locker, and he said Stash represented all those things that had lost their essence, and that's why we had to do away with him. George, who liked the idea from the start—but from a purely scientific perspective, as he kept reminding us—suggested killing the psycho-monkey instead, but Jun got really mad about that and said didn't we understand anything and said the monkey was the only animal at Critterworld worth living.

Jun had gotten the idea from a story we read in another advanced class on World Literature. It was that Japanese book, *The Sailor Who Fell from Grace with the Sea*, which I personally hated but which Jun read about ten times and carried with him everywhere like a bible. It was about a bunch of kids who dissected their cat because he didn't catch mice anymore, and later they dissected a sailor, I think because he was dating their mom. That was when Jun decided he was an ascetic, which he said made plenty of sense because his family was Catholic and the Catholics had an ascetic tradition of sitting in the desert and fasting and wearing hair shirts, and Jun said he saw a connection between that and the Japanese ascetics, which was what he said those kids were in the book, and he went on his own fast for purification, which lasted a couple of days until he went to bed one night and slept through all of the next day and the next night too, and his parents took him to the emergency room thinking it had something to do with his hemophilia.

Jun said he had a visionary dream about knocking off Stash during his two-day sleep, and he convinced George and me to learn

everything we could about elephants. He said we had to understand what Stash was supposed to be to experience the tragedy of
what he was instead.

At first I went along because Jun was so persuasive and because
he said all we had to do was kill Stash, not dissect him. Plus it was
usually easier to do what Jun wanted than to talk him out of it,
and besides, he often lost interest in projects before we saw them
through to the end. So we read the elephant book. We discussed
elephant lore. We figured out that Stash was an African elephant
rather than an Asian elephant—bigger ears—which I was happy
about once I learned how they trained elephants to work in India,
which was to make a hole in the back of their skull and poke inside
the hole with an iron bar.

Studying Stash himself was my idea. We were having a hard
time coming up with a way to kill him; George, in an uncharacter-
istically stupid moment, recommended dynamite, Jun said poison,
and I suggested gathering firsthand data on the subject while we
tried to figure it out. Jun agreed because, as he put it, we needed to
become more elephant than the elephant. And of course the idea
appealed to the scientist in George, who must have been the most
empirical guy in the state.

So that's what we were doing when Stash died—or what I was
doing. Jun just shrugged about it later and said it was coincidence;
he said Stash saved us a lot of trouble by dying when he did, but
something in his voice sounded false, and I wondered if maybe he
wasn't more upset than he was letting on. His mother let him paint
a St. George and the Dragon mural on his bedroom wall, which

seemed to take his mind off ritual slaughter for a while, and then we took up the Russians in that World Literature class and Jun decided to become a humanitarian.

My mother believes in God, which means she has a stock answer for things that can't be explained, and I go to church with her every week thinking one day it will rub off on me, too. She said God was watching out for us by taking Stash, but I still have my doubts.

After two hours trapped in the VW under Stash the little girl started squealing again—*Hreeee, hreeee, hreeee*—and nothing her mother or her father said could get her to stop. The sheriffs were useless, talking on their radios, calling more and more sheriffs to come out. They tried pulling Stash off with a wrecker truck, but that didn't work, and they were afraid he might shift and crush the car worse if they jerked at him hard.

Finally, though, Mr. Funderburke, the guy who owned Critterworld, got Steve's Sod Farm to send over three tractors, and together they were able to drag Stash off the car. The welder burned the girl's arm with his blowtorch cutting through the metal, but just a little, just a spark, and the sheriffs took the whole family to a motel in town, compliments of Critterworld.

Now the problem was what to do with the body. It became like a big joke there in the Critterworld parking lot: people saying, "How do you get rid of a dead elephant?" then cracking up, as if it was the funniest thing in the world. Stash must have weighed a couple of tons.

Woody Riser, the tree-service man, finally showed up with the biggest chainsaw I've ever seen. He consulted with the sheriffs and with Funderburke, then he lugged his chainsaw over next to Stash. The sheriffs herded everybody back a ways—there must have been a hundred people by then, and more coming all the time—and they formed a line around the body. Woody Riser mixed gas and oil for his tank, slipped on his safety goggles, then pulled the cord. On the third pull it coughed around and caught, and the noise was so loud that the little kids covered their ears. He went for a leg first, aiming carefully just above the knee where the skin was taut, but I guess he should have checked how tough the flesh was because the chainsaw kicked back on him and took a bite out of Woody Riser's own leg.

Things got a little crazy after that.

A couple of sheriffs put Woody Riser in their car and left for the hospital, and the rest of the sheriffs gave up on crowd control while they huddled with Funderburke to figure out what to try next. Right away people started pushing close to Stash. They all wanted to touch him, but some pulled out knives and poked at him with their blades. I saw a guy sawing at Stash's tail, and a couple of kids tugging on a tusk. Somebody else went for a piece of the ear.

George and Jun stood next to the psycho-monkey cage—the monkey had gotten hold of a cigar and they were watching him try to smoke it—but I didn't want to have anything to do with them for a while. I wanted to leave, but I also wanted to stay, and it was about then that I saw Sharla, that cheerleader from my Advanced Geometry class, standing by herself at the edge of the crowd.

I went over to her and stood there for a couple of minutes

before she noticed me. "Oh, hi, Charlie," she said. Her eyes were red from wanting to cry, but she hadn't cried yet. I tried to think of something to say back to her—something sensitive or clever—but nothing came except, "How's your geometry?"

She didn't have a chance to answer, though, or to laugh in my face and tell me how stupid I was, because a couple of pickup trucks pulled into the crowd and a bunch of football players from the high school got out with axes. "Elephant patrol!" they shouted. Everybody laughed except for me and Sharla, and the crowd pulled back to give the guys room to operate. Even the sheriffs seemed to think it was pretty funny, and they ignored Funderburke, who started yelling at them to stay away from Stash. "He can be stuffed," Funderburke kept saying. "He can be stuffed." Nobody listened.

"Isn't that your boyfriend?" I asked Sharla. I thought I recognized one of the football players.

"Oh, David wouldn't do that," Sharla said, obviously worried that David would. "He's just with them. He wouldn't—"

One of the football players climbed onto the hood of his truck and shouted: "County High one time!" The crowd roared, and an ax ripped into Stash's side.

"County High two times!" Another ax sliced the trunk.

"County High three times!" Two football players—one of them Sharla's boyfriend—hacked at Stash's legs.

"County High all the damn time!"

They attacked.

It must have gone on for a long time, guys passing off the axes when they got tired, always somebody new to step in for a few whacks at Stash. A couple of people left, offended, but more came, and the Critterworld parking lot turned black with blood. I didn't see too much, though, because I followed Sharla across the highway where she sat and cried in the ditch where George and Jun and I had been.

I'd never seen a girl that upset before, and I didn't exactly know what to do, so I just patted her on the back like my mother used to do to me when I was little. I wanted to tell her that her sorry boyfriend didn't deserve her anyway, but that didn't seem quite appropriate even though it was true. She cried harder and harder, but nothing could block out the thwack of axes or the pep rally cheers as they worked over Stash in front of Critterworld. I heard the psycho-monkey screaming, too, and figured he'd gotten to the ash-end of his cigar, and then, after a long time, just about when I started thinking I should leave Sharla alone because I was probably just bugging her, sitting there patting on her like I was, she turned her face to my shoulder and she cried onto my T-shirt and I put both of my arms around her as far as they would reach, and we stayed like that for a while longer until it was all over and nearly dark and a couple of her girlfriends came looking for Sharla to give her a ride home.

She wiped her eyes and climbed into the car, and she said something to me through the back window, but they were already pulling away so I didn't catch it. Maybe it was just "Good-bye" or "See you in class," or maybe she just said my name.

Pretty soon I was the only one left, sitting there in the ditch, except for Mr. Funderburke, who just stood in the parking lot like the broken man he was. The crowd was gone, the sheriffs, the football players with their axes, even George and Jun. I got up slowly and walked back across the road to get a last look at what was what. But now here's the really funny part: For all their chopping and their pep rally and everything, Stash was still there. Sure, he was cut to hell and bleeding everywhere, and his trunk and his tail were gone, and the ears were tattered and all like that, but he was still there. They could have swung their axes for another whole day and Stash would still have been there. Even dead he was too much elephant for them, and I wished Jun was there for me to show him, and to tell him that, and to make him understand.

They got those sod farm tractors back the next day and dragged Stash into a field behind Critterworld. They got a bulldozer and dug a big hole and dropped him in on a bed of wood soaked in gasoline. The fire lasted all night, and I got my mother to drive me out to see it. There were cars all up and down the road.

Some people say that Stash haunts that field now, that somebody stole his trunk and he looks for it on full moons, that passing motorists have seen him standing at three A.M. on his old spot in front of Critterworld. All that standard ghost story stuff. They even say that nothing will grow on the spot where Stash was cremated, but I guess you can write that off as rumor, too, because I've been out there a couple of times since and the grass is as green there as anywhere.

# Bocky-Bocky

He wasn't the handsomest drowned man in the world, but he wasn't bad looking, either, though little fishes had chewed out his eyes, leaving the sockets mournful and raw. He'd only been in the ocean about twelve hours, so he wasn't bloated, thank god. His skin was as gray as the early morning—it was five A.M. when Sam Witcher found him in the shallow surf—and the color had drained from his face. He had a pleasant enough smile, like a man who had just found a five dollar bill on the sidewalk, and though there was a suggestion of flab, he seemed to be in a perpetual state of sucking in his gut so that it didn't really show. Sam was happy to see that the drowned man still had his swimming trunks on. There had been speculation the day before that the man who drowned had been swimming off the nude beach between Robert Moses State Park and the town of Kismet, where Sam and his daughter Zoe and Zoe's friend Katy were staying with friends. Sam had walked down there once and seen a procession of older men with sagging waists and atrophied genitals and worried that he might be looking into his own future. One man, a transsexual, sat alone on a towel, his breasts hanging to his belly, his legs drawn up exposing his bald vagina. Sam got out of there as fast as he could.

Now he scanned the beach for signs of a lifeguard truck, and he strained to see through the fog and the still rough surf for the Coast Guard vessels that had crawled back and forth since the afternoon before. The storm had passed during the night, but Sam, waking every hour to see if Zoe and Katy were home yet, kept seeing the search lights from the deck of their beach house, so knew the rescue workers and the Coast Guard had pressed on through everything, through the barking wind and the howling rain and the dancing whitecaps and the churning foam. Where they had gone off to now was a mystery.

Sam pulled the drowned man far enough up the beach so the waves couldn't get him again, surprised, and grateful, at how easy that turned out to be, either because the man was lighter than he looked or because Zoe had gotten Sam to start lifting weights a couple of months before, which he still hated. Finally, he thought, a payoff. He arranged the body just so: legs straight, knees soft, arms down, palms up, shoulders relaxed, head straight, eyes, or what should have been the eyes, turned to the dark and overcast sky. It reminded Sam of a yoga pose—*savasana,* the Corpse. He looked at the drowned man for a long time. He knew he should run up to the beach house and call 911, but he didn't want to leave, either, because what if a tidal surge took the body while he was gone?

He sat down next to the drowned man. Then, although Sam didn't know why—gravity, fatigue, all those yoga classes over the three years since his wife, Anne, had passed away—he lay back in the wet sand in a *savasana* of his own.

It was quite the irony, Sam finding the drowned man. Earlier, watching the rescue boats, he had wished he could be one of the men onboard, standing bravely in rain gear, holding on to safety ropes, riding out the chaos of waves, studying the dark Atlantic for the terrible thing they knew was there somewhere. He had wondered if they kept up some hope that the drowned man might still be alive, might manage to tread water in a Zen state of calmness and acceptance until the time came for him to look up from the trough between twenty-foot swells into a bouncing searchlight and say, "Thank god you're here. I don't think I could have held on another minute."

But at least Sam had been the one to find him, and that was good, since it might be something to impress Zoe, something they could talk about. He lifted his head to look up and down the beach again. There was still no one. Just him and the drowned man. Sam closed his eyes and settled back into his *savasana*. When Zoe was little she had an imaginary friend named Bocky-Bocky. Zoe and Bocky-Bocky played a secret game in the faint surf of the Gulf of Mexico, where they lived back then. It involved a lot of whispering, then ducking under waves, singing to waves, admonishing waves, and once, when she didn't know Sam was watching, pulling down her suit and pooping in the waves. Zoe was sixteen now. Her life, which Sam had known intimately since she was born, was opaque to him. Everybody she met might as well be Bocky-Bocky for all he knew.

The girls had left at ten during a break in the storm to walk the quarter mile over to the bay side of the island, to The In and The Out, a couple of Kismet restaurants that doubled as all-night clubs. They were supposed to be back by midnight, but Sam didn't see them again until three when he climbed up to the widow's walk for a better look around. Two boys were walking Zoe and Katy back to the beach house up the narrow path between houses, and Sam was relieved until they stopped a block away to do some last things in what they thought was the cover of enough night and two giant umbrellas.

He got a side hug from Zoe, that and a whiff of a boy's cologne when she and Katy finally came inside. Katy said she was sorry, they lost track of the time, etc. "We'll talk about this in the morning," Sam said. Zoe sighed hard and edged past him downstairs to the catacomb of bedrooms and halls and bathrooms and closets that he still hadn't been able to entirely figure out, just as he wasn't entirely sure how many others had shares in the beach house. People were always coming and going, and he was pretty sure some of them were hooking up down there. He just hoped the girls weren't aware of it. He'd caught them drinking a beer the day before. At five, Sam went for a walk on the beach and found the drowned man.

Sam and the dead man had been lying side by side in the Corpse Pose for half an hour when somebody finally showed up, but it wasn't the lifeguard truck, it was the actress Uma Thurman. He heard her before he saw her—a "Fuck, fuck, fuck!" of discovery, then hyperventilation she choked off when he opened his eyes and sat up. She backed away stumbling as if she was going to faint into the surf, and Sam said, "Wait. Wait. I'm not dead. Just him."

"Goddamnit," she said. "You asshole. You scared the fucking crap out of me." Sam was surprised by the thick New York accent: "You ass-whole. You sked the fucken crap outta me."

Uma's eyes cut from Sam to the drowned man, to the drowned man's eyes. To what the fishes had done. She was a couple of inches taller than Sam, and she wore running shoes, shorts, a gray baggy sweater, and a baseball cap jammed down tight over her yellow hair. He wasn't surprised, exactly, that she was there, because the girls had seen her three days earlier on the ferry over from Bay Shore, traveling with a little girl and a nanny, but no sign of the actor-husband, whose name none of them could remember. The girls had told Sam she was more beautiful in real life than in the movies, even without makeup on, and it was so obvious she hadn't done anything to her hair, just tied on a scarf, and had he seen that pink poncho thing she was wearing, that awful thing with the fringe?

Sam said he was sorry for frightening her. Uma gestured toward the dead man. "Is he the one from yesterday?"

Sam nodded. Everyone had heard the helicopters and seen them hovering over the waves until the storm grew too intense and chased them back over to the Coast Guard station. People had come out of their beach houses and huddled in little clusters all up and down the beach.

Uma looked around. There was no one anywhere—just she and Sam and the drowned man and the sigh and crash of the sea. The sky behind her had lightened and the fog was beginning to lift, but it was still an hour before sunrise. Sam said again that he was sorry for scaring her. Uma crossed her arms and hugged herself. "What were you doing down there?" she asked. "Why were you lying there like that?"

Sam didn't know what to say, and he felt caught, the way he felt when Zoe demanded answers in that imperious way of someone who has been horribly wronged: Why had he embarrassed her? Why hadn't he told her how sick her mom was? Oh Jesus, who died from lung cancer anymore—especially if they didn't even smoke? Sam didn't know the answer to any of those things, and he didn't know why he had lain down in *savasana* next to the drowned man— except maybe that the guy just seemed lonely. So he said that.

Uma looked at him doubtfully. She looked at the drowned man. She looked back at Sam. He had been excited before, even proud that he was the one who found the drowned man, as if he had done something significant, something heroic. He hadn't really been afraid of a tidal surge; he didn't even know what a tidal surge was. He had been afraid someone else might come along and get the credit for finding the drowned man. And he'd been right to worry about that. If he'd left, it would have been Uma Thurman—Uma Thurman! As if she needed it.

She pulled off her baseball cap. She had a red line across her forehead from wearing it too tight. Sam wanted to suggest she loosen the band—it was the sort of thing he was always saying to Zoe and that Zoe was always ignoring—but he supposed she must have had to jam it on like that because the wind was still blowing so hard down the beach.

"When did they say they would get here?" she asked.

"Who?"

"Who you called." Uma wiped her face on her sleeve. Sam guessed she must hear compliments all the time and wondered if she was as dismissive with them as Zoe was with compliments he gave her.

"I didn't call," he said. "I didn't want to leave the body after I found him, so I thought I would just stay until somebody showed up."

Uma looked doubtful again.

"Do you want to call?" Sam asked. "Is your place near here?"

She looked back up the beach. "I was jogging."

He could tell she didn't want to call either.

"Look," he said. "I know who you are. And if this is a problem for you, I can just take care of it. I know you probably don't want the publicity and all that."

"What are you talking about?" Uma said back.

Sam shrugged. "You know."

"No." She planted her hands on her hips. "I don't know."

Sam folded his arms in front of his chest. She sure didn't have to get like *that* about it. "OK, I'm staying with the body. You can go call, you can go jog, whatever. I'm waiting right here for the lifeguard truck."

Uma snorted. "Is that right? Well I have just one question. The same question from before. What were you doing down there in the sand? Why were you lying down by that poor guy? Was there something funny going on?"

Sam felt very tired again. "No," he said. "There was nothing funny going on. It was a yoga pose. I just put him in a yoga pose. And then myself also."

"Yoga?" Uma said. Sam nodded. He stuck his hands in his pockets. Uma looked hard at the drowned man. She walked slowly around the body. She knelt by the head and brushed sand off the dead man's face.

"You mean *savasana?*" she said. "You were doing the *savasana* with the dead guy?"

"Yeah, yeah. *Savasana.*"

"The Corpse Pose?"

"Yeah, that's right."

Uma smiled and pulled her hands up into *namaste.* "The Corpse for the corpse. You could have told me this in the first place, you know."

"Ah." Sam waved his hand, relieved. "It was stupid. I don't know why I did it. I just found him. I was out for a walk because of worrying about my daughter. I wasn't thinking clearly."

Uma said she could see how these things might get mixed up in somebody's head. "I also have a daughter," she said. "She's back at the beach house with the nanny. That's why I have to jog so early and do my yoga practice. Once she's up, I'm all hers at the beach. What a little princess, let me tell you." She sighed. "Her father. Right now he's not with us."

Sam said he was sorry about that. The abrupt change in Uma's tone had him a little dizzy. He thought about telling her that Zoe had lost her mother and that he, too, was a single parent, but the therapist had said it wasn't a good idea to keep talking about Anne after this long, after Sam had so successfully cleared all the stages of grief, probably in record time.

"Some people," Uma said. "I won't mention names but, yes, it could include a certain father of a certain princess—they're so unawares I have to tell you. They take in the air, but they don't know how to breathe. It's what the yogis say: 'Where there is no breath, there is no life.'"

"I can see that," Sam said. He wasn't actually sure he could, but he wanted to be polite. He introduced himself, and she said, "Nice to meet you, Sam."

Then Uma turned her attention back to the drowned man. "His poor eyes," she said.

"I know," said Sam.

"It could be a blessing though," Uma said. "In a way."

Sam said, "It could?"

Uma nodded. "Where his mind is now, you probably see better without the eyes. Also, as a practical matter, in *savasana,* for deep relaxation and meditation, you don't need eye pillows to block out the light."

"OK," said Sam. He hadn't expected this, but he supposed you had to figure someone like Uma Thurman might see things differently from ordinary people like himself.

Uma asked exactly how long the drowned man had been in Corpse Pose. Sam pointed out that the man actually *was* a corpse, but Uma just said, "Of course, but how long in the *pose?* Maybe we should try a different *asana.* For example, did you consider the Child Pose?"

"Excuse me?" Sam said.

"Child Pose," Uma said. "After all he's been through, for recovery and restoration. To relieve the lower back strain from treading water and the violence of the waves. Child Pose could help with this."

"But he's dead," Sam said, as if he needed to keep reminding her of the fact.

Uma shrugged. "You said yourself he looked lonely. To me he looks tired. Just because he drowned doesn't mean he doesn't need the right *asanas*."

Sam knew there must be a hundred arguments against this, but he couldn't think of any fast enough. He looked nervously up and down the beach for sign of the lifeguards but saw no one, and the next thing he knew he was helping Uma lift the body. It felt even lighter than when he had pulled the drowned man out of the surf. Also rigor mortis hadn't set in as far as Sam could tell, so they had an easy time of it, first bending the knees to kneel the dead man on the ground, then folding his torso over his thighs until his forehead touched the packed sand. They drew his arms out in a sort of salaam in front of his body.

"OK," said Sam. "So that's it. That's the Child Pose." But Uma wasn't satisfied.

"Turn his face to the right," she said. "In Child I think you should start with the face facing the right." Sam did what she told him, careful not to touch the eye sockets. On the one hand, this was all very strange. On the other hand, who would have thought Uma Thurman would turn out to be a yoga master with such a deep compassion for the corpses of the dead? Although it did occur to

Sam that she might also be the kind of person who let herself get a little carried away with things.

Uma squatted in front of the dead man and lifted one of his arms. "There's still some strain in his shoulders," she said. "I think we should put him in *Sleeping* Child." Once again Sam went along. They pulled gently until the shoulders relaxed and the arms were stretched out long next to the torso, hands by the dead man's feet, palms cupped toward the sky.

"He's very flexible," Uma said admiringly. "What I wouldn't give to be so flexible."

"He must have really worked at it," Sam said.

"Work?" Uma said. "No. You gotta be in the moment, Sam. Progress is spontaneous. You can't make it happen."

A ghost crab poked up out of the sand next to the dead man's nose.

One thing led to another. That's all Sam could tell himself later to explain how he and Uma themselves came to be in Mountain Pose and the other *asanas* that followed. Mountain, as far as Sam had ever been able to tell, was just standing still with your eyes closed, only if you thought about it too much you lost your balance and fell. That didn't happen with him and Uma, though. The wind, which might have pushed somebody over before, had died down. They stood in Mountain for a good five minutes, their feet dug into the flat sand on the beach, and practiced their *ujjayi* breathing while the dead man stayed in Child. Uma was a lot more advanced than Sam and gave him plenty of advice. "If you want to increase your *prana* you gotta unlock your *mula bandha,* Sam. At the end of the breath, the total end of the breath, you feel the anal sphincter muscle contract, and it pulls your genital region upwards. That's how you know."

Next were the Sun Salutes, *surya namaskara.* Uma insisted. Not to worry, she said. The lifeguards would come when they were ready. Sam wasn't sure if by *they* she meant the lifeguards, or if she meant herself and him and the drowned man. Uma peeled off her sweatshirt, wrapped it around her baseball cap, and lay the bundle next to the drowned man. They faced the ocean. "Nine *vinyasas,* Sam," she said. "You ready? Five Sun Salutes?"

Sam said he guessed so, even though he didn't know what a *vinyasa* was. He wasn't too sure about the *prana* and the *mula bandha,* either, but Uma didn't give him time to ask before launching into the first Sun Salute. He followed tentatively, still stiff from the long night and the damp morning. He felt it most in his hamstrings so went easy on the Down Dogs and Bends, but Uma must have been made of rubber. He cheated a look and saw her face pressed into her knees for the first Forward Bend, and her heels stretched flat to the ground on Dog.

When they finished, Uma turned the dead man's head so he faced left, which was north up the island into the thinning fog of the morning. "We don't want his neck to stiffen up," she said. Then she and Sam did everything else—Triangle and Revolving Triangle, Half-Lotus Bound and Warrior, Head of the Knee and Boat. They even got deep down in the sand for Tortoise, or at least Uma did. Sam slipped into Child next to the drowned man. They'd been going at it a good half hour by then, and he needed the rest. While

Uma grunted through Tortoise he thought about Zoe back up at the beach house, Zoe with boys, Zoe when Anne came home from the hospital. There had been nothing more to do for her there. Anne's sisters came to help look after Anne and to say good-bye. Zoe was thirteen. Sam dropped her off at a friend's house one afternoon to hang out, and when he came back to get her he told her that her mom had passed away. Zoe blinked and blinked. Anne had been sick for so long, probably Zoe just thought she would always be that way. Zoe walked around the house a lot after that, not exactly looking for anything. Once Sam found her in a closet. He worried something was wrong with her, but she said she was just listening to music and there wasn't any other noise in there to distract her. She handed him her headphones. "Want to listen?" He put them on, but something must have messed up just then because all he heard was static.

The sun was pink behind the ocean when Sam and Uma finished with their yoga, and for a while Sam felt as if he were floating over the water, which was calmer now, like deep breathing. A fish jumped out of a wave. A dolphin rolled past and then three more. Sam imagined he was flying over the surf, through the spray and over the dunes and even back to the beach house where he had seen Zoe and Katy the morning before, lying head to toe in a single bed, snoring like babies.

When he opened his eyes Uma was checking out the drowned man again. She smiled and nodded at Sam, and he smiled and nodded back, resigned to whatever she wanted to do next. "Let's sit him up out of Child," Uma said, and they did. "Now bend his legs to Lotus," she said, and they did that too. Next they rolled his shoulders forward and rounded his spine. Sam brushed sand off the drowned man's back. Uma tucked his head down as far as it would go. They threaded his arms through his legs so the elbows hooked under his ankles. They pulled his forearms up and placed his hands on top of his head, then they stepped back to see what they had done.

"It's the *garbha pindasana*," Uma said. "The Fetus in the Womb. When you get so round like this, you can roll yourself down the beach like a bowling ball."

The lifeguards showed up a few minutes later in their white truck. A reporter was riding with them, although Sam and Uma didn't realize at first that's what he was. He had a digital camera in a plastic bag to protect it from the saltwater and air, and Sam read later that he got twenty thousand dollars for the photographs in a bidding war between the *Post* and the *Star*.

*How Twisted Is Uma? Film Femme and Friend Turn Drowned Man into Pretzel.*

The lifeguards asked questions about the finding of the body, and Uma made sure Sam got all the credit. They took turns explaining about the yoga. The lifeguards looked at them strangely. One said he had never seen anybody do *garbha pindasana*, dead or alive. The other lifeguard wrote everything down. The reporter, who had been silently taking pictures, asked if they were a couple and would they mind standing together next to the drowned man for a group shot. Up to that point they had thought he was just another lifeguard, but when he said that Uma started biting her nails. "Oh fuck," she said. "Paparazzi."

Sam didn't get it. "We're just friends," he told the reporter.

"How do you spell that name?" the reporter said.

Uma grabbed Sam's arm. "Ix-nay on the ame-nay," she said, and pulled her baseball cap low over her face.

"Hey," said one of the lifeguards. "Can you give us a hand over here?" All together they lifted the drowned man up, still in a ball, then carefully unfolded him in the back of the truck.

"Do you know who he is?" Sam asked.

"Not exactly," said the lifeguard. "There's five, six families—a whole bunch of people—all of them lost somebody and not just the one from yesterday. We got them still waiting from weeks ago. They're all back at the station. They all want to make the positive ID."

By the time Sam got back to the beach house the girls were already up. They were cooking pancakes. Zoe was in a good mood and called him Papa, which was something new. In the past it had always been Daddy, or Dad, or, more recently, just Sam. They couldn't have slept much—both girls had dark circles around their eyes—but he could tell they had washed their hair already. Zoe had French braids.

Katy handed him a cup of coffee. "I don't know what it's going to taste like, Mr. Witcher," she said. She pointed at the Mister Coffee. "I didn't know how much to put in."

Zoe flicked water on the griddle. "I don't know why I did that," she said to nobody in particular.

Sam said it was to see if the pan was hot enough for the batter. "Your mom always did it when she cooked pancakes. You thought it was funny."

Zoe said, "Oh yeah, I remember now."

A pop song came on the radio, and in an instant the girls were singing along. Sam tapped his spoon on the side of his mug. Anne and he used to sing like that in the kitchen, too, even though she had a voice like an angel and he couldn't carry a tune.

Zoe slid a big plate of blackened pancakes in front of him. "Even if they're no good you have to like them," she said. "Here's syrup."

"You made all this for me?" Sam said.

The girls looked at one another. "We invited the boys over for breakfast," Zoe said.

Sam asked, "What boys?"—as if he didn't know—and Zoe said some boys from last night they met at Kismet at the clubs. Sam remembered the widow's walk at three A.M., the break in the storm, the giant umbrellas. He sank onto his elbows at the table. He hadn't even had a chance to lecture Zoe and Katy about coming in so late, or to tell them about the drowned man and Uma Thurman. He had hoped his story would impress Zoe, make them closer as a father and a daughter. Now he wasn't so sure.

"They're in college," Katy said brightly. Zoe gave Katy a dirty look, then came over to kiss Sam on top of his head.

"It's OK, Papa," she said. "They're nice."

They talked about nothing for a while. They sang more songs on the radio. They made plans to visit the lighthouse. They waited for the boys. Sam finished up his pancakes and decided he would tell them about the drowned man later. And Uma. There wasn't any hurry, and it occurred to him that his story would only be a passing curiosity to Zoe anyway, no matter how interesting or strange—a distraction from her real life, a kind of appendix, a postscript, a footnote, and so would the other things lining up to happen in the weeks to come:

The tabloids the next day.

The other newspapers with their mean editorials.

The jokes on Leno and Letterman.

The midnight call from Uma, blaming him for wrecking her career.

Uma's out-of-court settlement with the family of the drowned man for the pain and the suffering.

The curious women at work who hadn't noticed him before, inviting him to dinners and movies.

The apology flowers from Uma, thanking him for boosting her career.

That night Sam dreamed about Anne, something that hadn't happened in more than a year. He dreamed she came to the foot of his bed and recited the Twenty-third Psalm. "The Lord is my shepherd, I shall not want." Sam listened sadly, then told her he thought he was a Buddhist so guessed he wouldn't be seeing her again in the afterlife. Anne said, "What you are, Sam, is sweet on that yoga teacher you met, the one that's the actress, and don't think you're kidding anybody about it." Sam said no he wasn't, and Anne said well he ought to be. Sam couldn't believe what he was hearing. Anne had always been so jealous, so possessive of him and Zoe, and so insecure, too. How could she change like this all of a sudden? He decided maybe it was a test.

"There's nobody but you," he said, choosing his words carefully, and it seemed to be the right thing, because Anne just laughed at him, though in a nice way, and said, "Oh, go on."

# Family of Man

Their black Turkana faces line Christoph's windows this morning like all mornings since he arrived in the northern bush. He stopped taking breakfast a year and a half ago because their yellow eyes were mirrors and their black teeth ground together while he chewed. They come with first light and would never leave if it weren't for the heat, and, later, for their night-fear of the djinn. He suspects that Cila, his housekeeper, gives away much of his food during the day while he supervises at the government *shamba*. He's seen cans flattened into plates, and he's seen children folding and cradling torn pictures of beans and corn and yams.

The Turkana lean on their spears. They stare at Christoph's hands, motionless in front of him on the bare wood table, huge clumsy red things that he thinks should belong to someone else. He has become self-conscious of his hands and wants to hide them, only there are too many Turkana in all directions pressed against the glass, and more behind the concrete walls that stand out so harshly here in the bush. Square is the wrong shape for desert, for thorn trees and sand and dying acacia.

They could come in, Christoph thinks—not for the first time—

as he dusts his fingers over his throat, touches his blue and white and ochre beads. They could kill him with their spears and take everything. He says this out loud, and Cila looks over from the gas stove, but she doesn't know English. He's talking to himself. People were afraid of the Turkana before the drought. Once, in Kapedo, at their southern border, Turkana warriors couldn't find any cattle on a raid against the Pokot, so speared Pokot children instead. Now, relief trucks and Finnish missionaries have bent Turkana and Pokot together there, lion and lamb.

Christoph spreads his Kenya map on the table, locates the blue brush stroke that marks the Turkwel, a finger of dry riverbed across central Turkanaland. An X next to the hard northern bend marks the government *shamba* and a ragged gathering of Turkana huts and kraals. Christoph has never seen water running in the Turkwel, and he knows the Turkana mark the distance to the few pockets of water underground there by the number of men it takes standing on one another's shoulders to reach that deep.

Cila brushes his elbow with her hip as she sets a cup of weak tea over the legend on a corner of his map. Today will be the last day he sees her, or any of the Turkana. As soon as he gets to Nairobi—two days' drive, because he has to travel northeast first, to Lodwar, for more petrol and to find the one road—he'll have fruit and sausages and eggs and that too-green Kenyan coffee with cream. He'll go at night to the French place, Alain Bobbe's, for grilled swordfish, and he'll sniff his wine before he drinks it, and he'll overtip the snotty European waiter to make up for the proper clothes Christoph doesn't own to wear to a place like that, and he'll go to the casino north of the white island, which is downtown, and he'll let a Kikuyu whore attach herself to him while he plays Judas Iscariot and gambles the bagful of shillings he collected for the Turkana well.

The last time in Nairobi—two months ago, when he drove in to get the hand pump and the pipe—he went to the Thorn Tree bar for beers with some UN people, and some International Voluntary Servicers, and a couple of Peace Corps types who'd been run off from their north coast village by Somali bandits. Christoph hadn't said much, because he hadn't used English in so long, and the others started calling him Kurtz.

The Peace Corps didn't get it. "How come they call you that?"

Even Christoph laughed, and the young Peace Corps reddened, and Christoph remembered how somebody described the PCs once as aggressively naive.

The UN ag agent, a Brit named Thompson, explained. "You stay out in the bush long enough, you get the savior complex. We ain't seen Chrissie here in six months, have we?"

Thompson lived outside Nairobi, in Nancy, in a walled compound with a guard who used poison-tipped arrows and last year had to shoot a man. Thompson said he watched the bandit break off the arrow just before the poison sent him into convulsions and he bit off his tongue.

It was Thompson who two years ago warned Christoph about the native women. Christoph had only been in country four months then, and his wife, Anna—pregnant, although she miscarried shortly after she got back to the States—had been gone a week. "Thompson's Rules," the Brit called them. "Number one: don't poke the housegirl. Number two: if you can't go to Malindi for it, settle for Mombassa, and if you can't make the coast towns, use your hand."

Christoph looks up from his map and watches Cila now move restlessly through the concrete house, silent on her bare feet, graceful with her long arms and legs that never seem to rest. She's the only Turkana woman he knows in the bush who seems alive, who has flesh that is taut, breasts that don't sag, a back straight and strong, not worn down by the hours the others spend with their heavy clay jars and their water treks that can take half a day—walking on hard feet to dry riverbeds farther and farther off, digging with their hands where they smell water or see traces of green algae, usually settling for mud and cloth and patient straining. It hasn't rained in Turkanaland in more than two years. Christoph's food and water, trucked here in barrels, are what keep Cila alive. For her he fantasizes waterfalls, ocean surf, crystal streams.

In Turkana he reminds Cila that he's traveling to Nairobi today, and she nods and disappears into the bedroom to pack his clothes. She thinks it's business, that he'll be back, but by this time next week he'll be out of country, home with Anna, if they still have a home— and he has to believe that they do. He won't be a Kurtz to these people or to himself. Marlowe maybe—only Marlowe traveled up the river of sand to find not malevolence but indifference: When it rains, jungles grow overnight. When there's drought, people die.

Christoph counts the faces, fewer of them now pressed against his windows, in the hot shade of his tin porch. The heat has already forced some of the older ones back to their huts. Some of the young men wait to see if Christoph will try the hand pump again on another shallow well. Some of the young women wander off to the government *shamba* to offer themselves to the Kikuyu soldiers under the shade trees past the cassava field. The diesel pump that irrigates the crops can drown their grunts and cries there, unless the soldiers have used all the fuel again, siphoning barrels to sneak the Land Rover into Lodwar for town whores and beer. They will hate Christoph when he takes the truck. They have little to do here fifty kilometers from town except guard the crops from Turkana thieves.

The big government *shamba* is a showcase to prove what aid money can do in the bush with a deep-well pump and fertilizer and hybrid seed and tractors. Only they're down to one tractor, because Christoph has had to pirate parts from the others for repairs, and the money the crops bring in Lodwar and Eldoret doesn't cover expenses, and they have jobs for only a handful of Turkana.

In Nairobi once, when Christoph complained about this, Thompson took him to a River Road warehouse, flashed his United Nations ID to a guard, and dragged back a metal door. Inside were a dozen elephant-sized combines—no, they were bigger than elephants: they were dinosaurs under a thick layer of red dust, still smelling of packing oil and sour straw. "Three years, Chrissie," Thompson said. "They've been here three years. Only we don't have any spare parts for them, either. No mechanics to work on 'em. No way to get 'em to the bush."

Christoph wanted to know who was in charge.

Thompson smiled and saluted.

• • •

Three of the younger men are tapping at the window by the door. One, who Christoph recognizes as Cila's brother, makes a pumping motion with his arm. The others pump, too, and in an instant a dozen more Turkana join them. An old man in a tattered leopard skin appears, and Christoph gets up immediately. He could wave off the young men, but ignoring the *mzee* would be too serious an insult.

Cila's brother is already lifting the red hand pump from the porch. The *mzee* points to the PVC pipe and the joints and tools, and others pile them onto their shoulders. Christoph leads the way into the sun with the old man at his elbow: if the *mzee* wants to try the well one more time, there's no way to refuse. But Christoph's body feels too heavy; every step is a struggle through the hot sand, and as they move from shade into desert heat he experiences the too-familiar tightening of his throat, nearly as dry in five minutes outdoors as if he hadn't had water for days.

Christoph had sidestepped Thompson, the UN, everybody, two months ago when he went to Nairobi for the pump. His plan— the plan he'd sold the Turkana after endless meetings with the *mzee*—was shallow wells, each enough to irrigate a one-family *shamba*. Start with a single pump, one *shamba*, one family, he told the *mzee*. Show people that the water is there, shallow enough to reach in small amounts so a hand pump can draw it up, can grow millet for one family. Then next year maybe two pumps. Next year maybe they close the government *shamba*, send the soldiers home, shut off the diesel pump, fill the deep well. Maybe then they buy hand pumps for all the Turkana.

The *mzee* sat and discussed this for weeks. Called Christoph back. Visited the site he and Cila's brother and the other young men had already cleared for the first *shamba*. Sat again. Finally decided: every family gives one shilling. When all shillings are collected, Christoph buys the pump.

The *mzunga* at the supply house in Nairobi, an old white guy from colonial times who said he used to safari with the great Bunny Allen, ended up giving Christoph the pump for free. Christoph kept quiet about it, though; the pump would mean more if the Turkana thought they'd sacrificed.

The first well two months ago came up empty. The second brought a trickle. It wasn't until the fifth try that the pump coughed out a brown stream of sour water. Christoph and the young Turkanas shouted and sang as they rushed ahead of the water, digging shallow channels with their hands to irrigate the cleared half acre. That afternoon the *mzee* ordered two goats slaughtered and bled to bless the new *shamba* ground, and they roasted the goat meat on an open fire in celebration. That well stopped producing after a day and a half.

There had been five more wells since then—the young men can't work for more than a couple of hours a day, as weak as they are from malnutrition, and as dry as they are in the heat—but none produced very long, either. Christoph realized they would have to go deeper, get more pipe, double their effort. With each new well and each new failure, he began to doubt what he had been so certain of before: that the water was there, shallow enough for hand pumps. If it was too deep, they'd never get it up, but if it was too close to the surface the wells tapped out in days.

Today they'll try a new site that the young Turkana spent last week preparing. They crowd around Christoph now, arguing about where to dig, where to sink the PVC, and once again— despite what he tells himself, despite all he knows: that hope is a curse—Christoph is struck by the possibility of the moment, and he is feverish, infected, thirsty for what could happen. The debate has become a part of the well ritual: the young men argue for half an hour while the *mzee* listens and nods and shouts a few ideas of his own. Finally, the *mzee* turns to Christoph, asks for his suggestion, and Christoph chooses a spot. Sometimes the *mzee* agrees with him, sometimes he doesn't. It's always the *mzee*'s call.

Really, they know so much more about water than Christoph does that he figures the *mzee* is just being polite by asking his opinion on where to dig. They must have fifty different words for water in the Turkana language, and Christoph still doesn't know them all: a word for those delicate beads of dew the Turkana lick off the acacia at first light, a word for those faint puddles that collect in tiny cisterns hidden among wind-sculpted piles of desert rocks, a word for the moisture that forms those rare clouds in the blue Turkana sky—clouds Christoph has grown to hate because on bad days he thinks they're the work of sinister gods who tease the Turkana by holding up a drink that people can see but never reach.

"Here then?" Christoph says to the *mzee,* motioning near the center of the field. But the *mzee* shakes his head. Today the *mzee* wants to divine a spot. He tells Christoph that the problems with the other wells were the fault of guesswork, or human error. They weren't able to read the signs properly, or they were too quick to clear and dig. Time to bring in one of the older *mzee* with the tools to select a site correctly. Christoph thinks about arguing, but the heat today and the failures over the past couple of weeks have made him uncertain. So why not trust in divination, incantation? Why not trust in kinder gods? Christoph nods. The *mzee* growls orders to one of the younger men who lopes off in the direction of Christoph's house and the village.

The rest move away from the field to squat in whatever shade they can find. While they wait, Cila's brother tells Christoph that a leopard took his uncle's two-year-old daughter a couple of nights ago, but Christoph isn't sure he believes the story. Cila has told him that some Turkana kill their own children now because there's nothing to give them once the mother's milk stops, and they often claim it was leopard death.

Christoph and Anna were three months out of ag school when they met their first Turkana. That was two and a half years ago at a military checkpoint on the dirt washboard Kenya-Sudan highway at the southern edge of Turkanaland. They were squeezed into the cab of their Land Rover with the Brit, Thompson, as they waited in 110 degree heat for a soldier in a tin-roofed hut to clear their papers. The road there was lined with metal shacks, and Christoph supposed it was a village, though it didn't have a name. All he knew was they were entering the Lotikipi Plain: nothing but thorn trees and sand stretching north to the Sudan border, east to the salt shores of Lake Turkana, and west to the mountains in Uganda.

The beggar appeared suddenly, inches from Anna's window, hand lifted, open. Christoph saw jaundiced eyes, black teeth, hanging rags of skin—saw Anna reaching into the food crate behind the seat until Thompson caught her arm. "You can't feed him," Thompson said. "They'll all come."

"All who?" Anna said, but Christoph could already see other black faces peering from the dark huts with those same yellow eyes.

Anna pulled out a box of wheat cereal anyway and gave the man some, which he stuffed into his mouth, pushed with long fingers past his swollen tongue. But he was too dry, he couldn't close his lips, and every time he worked his jaws the cereal fell until it lay at his feet in the sand.

In the back of the truck they carried water, beer, flour, *ugali*. The soldier wanted a case of beer before he would stamp their papers, so Thompson bargained quickly and they left that place, left the Turkana beggar standing where the truck had been, hand still raised, palm still open, as if he had more manna coming. An hour farther on they saw cattle skulls by the road, and, still farther, three women walking, two of them balancing water jars, the third bearing the severed head of a donkey.

By the time they reached the government *shamba* and the concrete-block house by the Turkwel, Christoph knew Anna wouldn't last. "What are we supposed to do?" she asked him, crying. That was the day they found a corpse on their porch. And every morning the Turkana came with first light, and every evening the night spirits drove them home again, and Anna crawled inside her mosquito net and dreamed she was flying.

Anna got pregnant after two months in Africa.

It happened during a week away from the government *shamba*—because her dreams about flying had turned into nightmares about falling—when they drove a hundred kilometers east of Lodwar to a camp on Lake Turkana. The families who fished the lake brought giant perch every morning, which the Britisher who ran the camp cooked for Christoph and Anna at night. They ate fish and drank beer and even swam in the saltwater after enough assurances that the crocodiles stayed on the far eastern shore.

A government subsidy kept the camp open, the manager said. Christoph and Anna were the first visitors in months; no one came north anymore since the drought. One of the local *mzee* repeated what the manager said: that Christoph and Anna were the first *mzunga* tourists at the camp. But the *mzee* had a different explanation: he said it was because of a devil living in the bottom of a small freshwater spring near the lake, and he said the Turkana would sacrifice a goat to feed the devil. When the devil was no longer hungry and no longer angry at being ignored, more tourists would come.

So they slaughtered the goat, bled it on the sand around the spring, sold the choice meat to Christoph and Anna, and threw the rest into the water.

They waited, but not long, because two days later a family of Texas Baptist missionaries showed up from Kitale driving a flaming red Jeep Cherokee and boasting that one of their converts was the wife of Kip Keino, the famous Kenyan runner. They were enthusiastic about everything: their new truck, their church, the prospect of getting Kip Keino into the congregation.

"He's still what you call an animalist," the father said.

"Animist," his wife corrected.

"But we're working on him," the father said. "And when he comes I predict he will bring many another."

The children fired cap pistols at some Turkana who were trying to sell them bead necklaces.

Christoph told the missionaries about the devil in the spring, but the father shook his head sadly. "They're living a lie," he said. "Prayer is the only thing that's going to help, whether it's Turkana, Pokot, Kikuyu, Samburu, or whatever."

"Amen," said the wife.

"Amen," said the children, who were busy handing out crosses to the Turkana.

"Amen," said Anna, and her laughter caught Christoph off guard. He had forgotten the sound. She laughed later, too, when they were alone, lying together on mats over the swept dirt floor of their open-sided cabana near the lake. She turned to him that night for the first time since coming to Turkanaland. "Play missionary with me," she said, and he didn't get it until she pulled him on top of her and whispered his name over and over until long after he was finished.

Anna must have known what would happen, Christoph has since realized. He was supposed to follow her to the States as soon as he could—once the government hired someone else to manage the *shamba*—but Anna miscarried after she was home in America, and she said she'd be back, and she never came back.

The young men sink pipe for two hours after the divination. Christoph directs, but he left his hat at the house earlier, and his ears and nose redden as the sun burns higher and bleaches the land of color. The desert world fuses into shades of white in the afternoon, and Christoph's eyes ache from trying to judge distance and form without the aid of shadows. And yet despite himself he still follows the work anxiously, harassed by a voice that insists: "Maybe this time. Maybe this is the one—"

A Kikuyu soldier materializes at the edge of the clearing, and Christoph asks him to bring the Turkana a bucket of water. If any of the Turkana approach the diesel pump themselves, the Kikuyu have orders to shoot, and Christoph can't leave the workers alone with the pump. The soldier looks past him, impassively. Christoph has no official military authority, so they often ignore him, but this one, perhaps interested in the *shamba* experiment, maybe just bored, finally agrees to go.

Christoph knows that most of the young Turkana, already out of hope for the shallow-well pump, help dig only on the chance of getting a taste of brown water from the soldiers, and once they get their drink it isn't long before they begin drifting off. He is angry anyway when it happens, though—angry for letting himself be so stupid, for wanting it, still, again: *this well, this time.* Even the *mzee* vanishes today after the soldier returns, and finally only Christoph and Cila's brother are left to carry the hand pump and the PVC to the concrete-block house.

Nothing ends here, Christoph thinks as they drag through the sand. It fades. Smoke in still air.

Cila has his rucksack full and laid out on the table with a jug of water and a sack of food. She has made a stew from canned things, she says, pointing toward a pot on the gas stove, but Christoph shakes his head. He looks around at all he's leaving and sees it's not much: some books, some pictures, some records from the government *shamba*. He rifles through the table drawer until he finds all his letters from Anna—every other week when she first left, only a couple over the last several months, none for a while. But when she sees him they'll be all right. Just the two of them. Of course they'll be all right. He folds the letters and his Kenya map and shoves them into the food bag.

Cila stands silently at the door as Christoph throws his gear into the Land Rover and flicks on the starter bulb for the diesel. Her face is a mask, betraying nothing, but even at that Christoph feels guilty. She knows, he tells himself, and the engine cranks, and a few Turkana appear from around the sides of the house to see him leave, fascinated as always by the magic of the truck.

He waves to Cila, but she doesn't wave back, and already she's fading, too, dissolving into the white light of the desert afternoon.

As he drives off, Christoph remembers the day, now more than two years ago, when he and Anna left their holiday on Lake Turkana. They had been driving silently for hours, first west, and then north toward Lodwar, when a glint of color made him stop. Anna cursed the dust that caught the Land Rover and choked her, but there, he saw, ten feet from the road, were the bleached skull and rib bones and thigh of a Turkana girl. He climbed from the truck, wondering if she had died there or if something had dragged her, but mostly wondering why *there*? The road they were on was a dirt track, a thin, red map line, and the Lotikipi Plain was a moonscape without end, a land baked and cracked and dry.

Christoph kneeled, and he touched the girl's thigh gently, like a lover, touched her blue and white and ochre beads. Without thinking, he slipped the necklace over his head, and it fit like skin. Anna must have seen this, too, when he climbed back into the truck. She handed him a hot Tusker beer, and together they toasted the victory of life over death.

# Desgraciado

A Chicano boy peeks into my car window while I wait for the signal to change at the end of the dusty off-ramp at the exit for Medical Center Drive. These boys are all so small; I can see only half of this one's face. "*Light?*" he asks me. "You want this *Light* today?"

The first time it happened, the day I arrived in Texas, I was confused and wondered if he was offering me a choice between cool night and dry, dust-choked day, a choice that couldn't exist, and I stared blankly at the forced smile and the wide brown face. The signal changed, and I accelerated away before seeing the stack of newspapers under the boy's arm and the change apron around his waist: *San Antonio Light.*

Today I buy a copy automatically, glance at the headlines for news of the hostage, toss it into the back seat with the others. They've been piling up for a week now, on my way to and from the hospital, and I keep meaning to bring them to the clerk in Special Medicine when I visit my mother. The clerk buys two copies every morning to play the Loteria, and I could double her chances if I only remembered to give her my papers too.

I drive off, finally, and wonder if they read the papers they sell—

these tiny boys who spend their Texas summers counting quarters and hustling the *Light*. I hope they don't, because the news has been so terrible. The headlines yesterday said forensic specialists think the hostage, the American businessman in the Middle East or Somalia or Ecuador—I keep forgetting—was already dead before he was hanged. Today's paper says his wife doesn't believe it's really him in the pictures, and she's asked the kidnappers for proof of his identity.

The Medical Center visitors' lot is already full, so I park under the mesquite trees in the red fire zone with a dozen other cars. They never ticket us here, they never tow us away. Probably nobody cares, because it's so hot in the Southwest this summer that fire would be as big a relief as rain. They've banned cigarettes from the hospital, so I have to pass through a circle of smokers who ring the building outside—some in street clothes, more in hospital gowns, others leaning on their IV poles.

I told my mother that crossing that nicotine line reminded me of playing Red Rover when I was little, and she said, "Red Rover, Red Rover, let Henry come over." The way it came out, though, her words slurred so badly I could hardly understand, made me try too hard to laugh, to convince her she was funny and her voice was OK. She put her left hand on my forearm to reassure me, but all that told me was the paralysis was receding. I knew she still couldn't feel anything.

I promise to be upbeat today, though, and on the way down to the Special Medicine ward I say *buenas días* to the clerk and to the Bexar County sheriff's deputy. The deputy, a dark, burly man who never sits and who seems too large for his brown uniform and for the corridor, has been here more than a week on twelve-hour shifts, watching the patient I call Desgraciado. The deputy's replacement, an Anglo, comes in at midnight. Last week when I asked why they were on the ward, the deputy nodded at the room across the hall and said, simply, "Guarding that godforsaken thing." He said it in Spanish, though: *desgraciado*—without grace.

Now something catches in my throat, like fingers tightening, cutting off air: Desgraciado himself is out of his bed and pressed inside against the door, his face inches from the reinforced glass window between the gray sign that says RESPIRATORY ISOLATION and the orange one that says NO FLUID CONTACT. He is so short, not much taller than the newspaper boys, that I can see only his hooked nose and his pocked brown cheeks and his silver hair and his yellow eyes glaring out at me in the hall.

Those small, jaundiced eyes frighten me—Desgraciado frightens everyone on the ward—yet for an instant I am paralyzed: like driving by an accident, I have to stop and stare. He's bloodless and powerful and evil. He was lieutenant of a Southwest heroin ring. Now he's under a death sentence with hepatitis and AIDS, the deputy tells me. "Whatever you can get from needles or from fucking."

I look away and hurry on to my mother's room.

"Henry." She says my name, barely slurring it this time, and I smile at the improvement. I have brought her a radio and a hairbrush. She keeps asking for a hand mirror, but I don't want her to see her face just yet, the way it sags since the stroke. I don't tell her how she looks, and I say nothing about Desgraciado under guard down the hall. It's important that I protect her from these things.

My mother was upstairs in her narrow two-story San Antonio townhouse the night she felt someone else in the bed. Her foot touched the stranger's leg, and she woke, panicked, in the dark. Something held her back as she struggled to get up, and she knew it was him. "Help me!" She remembers screaming, and her own screams gave her the strength to break free, then to reach for the phone. She didn't have her glasses, though, and a hand touched her arm and she broke away and stumbled down the stairs, that hand grabbing, trying to drag her back. She made it to the door, and to the neighbor's.

"Please," the neighbor heard her voice, desperate like a child's. "Please. Someone is trying to get me."

Later, at the hospital, the doctors explained everything. The stroke not only affected my mother's entire left side, they said, taking away all feeling and control, but also took away any awareness of that half of her body. *Hemi-neglect* was their word for it. The leg she felt in the bed, the arm that clawed at her going down the stairs—were my mother's own.

Because she was able to get to the hospital so quickly—the stroke still in evolution, the doctors said—they have included her in a blind study of an experimental drug, a miracle anticoagulant. She's either getting the miracle drug or she's taking a placebo, and we won't know for a year either way, but it's meant teams of neurologists and cardiologists and other specialists invading her room, stabbing her limbs, pinching her face, stealing her blood, kidnapping her for CAT scans and EEGs and ultrasounds and magnetic resonance imaging. They speak a language so specialized that I think the stroke itself is a thing alive, and I pore through medical dictionaries to learn the difference between aphasia, which my mother doesn't have, and apraxia, which she does. Together we fret over hemiplegia, which is paralysis on one side, and hemiparesis, which is merely weakness, which we would prefer. The doctors speak almost admiringly about my mother's clot, which they say was the size of a half-dollar. The stroke itself they call a "cerebrovascular accident," which seems utterly inappropriate to me: an accident, as if she'd been struck by a drunk driver like the girl in the next bed, who can't speak or open her eyes, but does finally, after weeks in a coma, squeeze her father's hand when her father begs long enough and loud enough.

Nothing here was accidental, I want to tell the doctors. There's a reason for everything. Look at your own goddamn literature: her cholesterol was high, she drank too much sometimes, and she used to smoke. She was under a lot of stress at work. She had atherosclerosis—another one of your words that means too much fatty deposit clogging her artery walls.

She was supposed to have a stroke.

Late into the experimental program I asked about the miracle drug: where it came from, what exactly it was supposed to do. What they told me was that the miracle drug has a special thinning agent that dissolves existing clots more effectively than other treatments and helps blood slip through narrowed arteries so there's less chance of future clotting. What they also told me—and I couldn't help thinking they were kidding at first—was the drug is a venom extract from Malayan pit vipers.

The father of the girl in the next bed wants to get Desgraciado off the ward. He has a petition he wants me to sign. "I'll take it to the hospital administration," he says. "If that doesn't work, we'll go to the City Council. I already talked to the sheriffs, and they're no help at all."

I tell him I'm not from San Antonio, I'm from Florida, but he says that shouldn't matter. "Call me Bob," he says. I tell him to call me Henry. My mother is asleep, and we're standing by Bob's daughter's bed, looking out the window. Heat rises visibly off the rooftops below us, and cars down on the street appear twisted and distorted, all wrecked in the distance through the shimmering air.

"That guy, he could get out," Bob says. "I've seen him at the door, studying the guard like he's waiting for his chance. And that guard doesn't always stand right there in the hall. I've seen him down at the desk sometimes. He's talking Spanish with the clerk and the nurses.

"We've all been through enough without having to worry about scum like that. The newspapers said he cut out a woman's tongue who was going to testify against him. I say put him in a prison hospital. Let him take his chances. Let them worry about him there."

Bob's voice trembles as he speaks. Last night when the curtain was drawn between the beds I heard him crying. He must have been sitting on his daughter's bed—Star is her name—and he was saying, "Open your eyes, Star. Open your eyes, baby. Squeeze Daddy's hand."

I sign the petition.

At the hospital the next day, Desgraciado is at his door, tapping, trying to draw the deputy's attention. The deputy motions him back with his night stick, then pushes the door open a crack, and curses in Spanish. Desgraciado retreats to a chair under the television in his room, but he stares out toward the hall the whole time and he sees me there watching. I avert my eyes and slip away down the corridor.

My mother is talking long distance to my sister in Boise, and I'm surprised at how normal her voice sounds. She waves to me stiffly with her left hand. The wrist doesn't bend and the fingers don't move, but she's obviously proud that she's able to wave at all. I motion for her to keep talking, and I step past the curtain to see if Bob is visiting his daughter and to see if he's gotten anywhere yet with our petition.

Star is alone in her bed, her eyes closed tightly under the deep purple spider-bruise on her forehead—the only visible mark from her accident except for a broken leg, which is hidden under white hospital sheets. Star's foot, the one on her good leg, is tapping out a beat to no music I can hear, and she makes a feeble drumming motion with a couple of the fingers on her right hand. Neurological damage may be the cause, but for all anyone really knows she could be spending a lazy afternoon lying here, humming to herself, playing with melodies in her head.

"Hi, Star," I whisper, as if she might open her eyes and smile and say sorry, she was just resting and didn't know anyone was coming by. "I'm a friend of your father's, Star," I say, thinking the petition *is* a sort of bond between Bob and me. We're both trying to get Desgraciado off the ward for Star's sake and for the sake of my mother and the other patients. "Your father has been worried about you," I say. "He's been here every day trying to get you to open your eyes."

She moans, and rocks in her bed, then settles into the valley of her mattress. Her lips are chapped, and I dip a washcloth into a pitcher of water the way I've seen the nurses do, and I wipe softly, squeezing so that a little water dribbles into her mouth. Her throat shudders, an involuntary act of swallowing. My mother is still on the phone on the other side of the curtain.

I lean in close over the bed, and my own lips are inches away as I whisper into Star's ear. At first it's just hospital talk: my mother in the next bed, the Malayan pit viper venom, the nurses, the smokers outside. I tell her about current events, the hostage in the *Light,* the size of the Loteria. I tell her about my job—I work in newspapers, too—and about my wife, Rennie. We met in journalism school and got married after we landed jobs on the same paper as reporters. That was back in Florida. She was hungry to cover everything, explain it all, but it made me too nervous—the interviewing, the deadlines, the relentless pace of the news.

I moved out of reporting and into an editing position for awhile, but that wasn't far enough away. I was still nervous. Finally I took a graphic design job in the advertising department. That separation they always insisted on between the news and business operations became a personal wall between me and Rennie, though, and when she landed a better job in Atlanta she moved up there alone. Ever since then I've been spinning out of whatever current it was that carried me while we were together. I couldn't say where Rennie and I were going, exactly—we never discussed children—but she gave me a kind of structure, anyway, something I'd been without since my own family drifted apart: my mother alone here in San Antonio, my father remarried and living in California, my sister with daughters and an engineer husband in Idaho, my brother engaged to a Belgian woman and stationed in Germany. Actually, *drift* might not be emphatic enough to describe what happened to us, or what we did to ourselves—and there's water in my voice, I realize, and I've been leaning in close the whole time, saying all of this out loud to Star.

"*Atomized*," I say. "*Atomized* might be the better word."

At the hospital a day later I hold my breath to lunge through that circle of smokers outside, and I have a light-headed sensation of not breathing again until I'm up the elevator and down the Special Medicine corridor. I pause at Desgraciado's door. The deputy is inside leaning against a wall, thumb hooked under the leather strap of his gun holster. Desgraciado is cutting the air with his finger, stabbing out and up as he talks to a man in a suit, an Anglo who sifts through papers in a briefcase laid open on the bedside table. Desgraciado sits on the bed, the Anglo stands, the deputy shifts his weight from one foot to the other. Maybe they hear me, or maybe they sense I'm there, as if they've been expecting me. The three men turn toward the hall. Desgraciado fixes his thin mouth into a smile like a stiletto, and I hurry on to my mother's room, away from his accusing, yellow eyes.

My mother is downstairs in radiology, though—gone for yet another EEG—so I step around the curtain to the other side of the room, thinking maybe Bob will be there but hoping I'll have another opportunity to be alone with Star.

And sure enough, there she is: also waiting for me, I can't help think, as if she'd just had the nurses scrub her clean for my visit. Her eyes are closed, but not too tightly, her face is flush with color, her hair is brushed and fanned out on the pillow, and that spider-bruise looks softer now on her forehead. Not like a wound, but like a sign, maybe. Like God's purple kiss.

I kneel beside her.

"Star," I say. "It's me, Henry, and I'm back."

In the days that follow I look for more opportunities to be alone with Star. I pretend it's because she might need me, but there's something else, too, something safe in our being together. Sitting with my mother leaves me afraid—or worse, vulnerable: thinking about Desgraciado, seeing his troll face, straining to hear his fingers rake the door. I time my visits for when I know my mother will be downstairs in tests or in therapy. Star's father goes with her some-times, and sometimes he waits for me to collect signatures for the petition to get Desgraciado off the ward.

I spy on Desgraciado every day. I make up excuses to talk to the deputy so I can see him more clearly in the back of his room, sitting in the blue chair under the wall TV. More and more often, though, Desgraciado is a sentinel at his own door—pressing his face to the window, studying the hallway, owning us with his yellow eyes.

By the end of the week Bob and I have gathered thirty signatures, and we finally meet with one of the hospital administrators in an office downstairs with glass walls looking out over a much larger room with banks of computer terminals and the backs of people's heads. The administrator reads our petition as deliberately as if he were examining a patient chart or checking for vital signs. He nods a lot, frowns to himself, twirls his pencil. Then he looks up and thanks us for our concern.

Bob rises from his chair. "What is that supposed to mean?" he says. "Does that mean you're going to do something, or does it mean you're blowing us off here?"

The administrator says it means they'll do what they can but that their hands are tied by a court order, and funding could be jeopardized if they were to refuse treatment, and they're sure the security is appropriate on the ward, and the patient poses no real threat—

But Bob cuts him off. "Look here, boy. You look right here. If that son of a bitch gets loose, if he does anything to my daughter or to this man's mother, if any goddamn thing happens, so help me—"

He's standing now, shaking his fist at the administrator.

"So help me—" Bob says it again, but he doesn't have the words to finish.

I touch his elbow. He's trembling. "Come on, Bob," I say, and I guide him toward the door. "Let's go. The hell with this guy. The hell with him. We can take shifts. Take turns spending the night in the room. We can make sure nothing happens ourselves. We can take care of them."

Later, Bob and I eat dinner together at La Fonda, a Mexican restaurant just off Medical Center Drive near the interstate. The waiters are all Hispanic; most of the diners are Anglo.

"Your mother, she seems to be doing a lot better," says Bob, who is my father's age. "I've spoken with her a few times the last couple of days, and you can see the improvement."

He asks what my mother does for a living. "I understand she's out here by herself," he says. I explain that she's assistant director of programs at the Alamo. When she first took the job my mother rewrote the tour guides' scripts to bring them in line with the work of modern Alamo scholars, and visitors were shocked to hear that Davy Crockett's wound might have been self-inflicted and that he was likely drunk and hiding when he was killed in Santa Ana's last, successful assault. And as for that line Colonel Travis was supposed to have drawn in the sand with his sword, well—

But the complaints nearly did her in, I tell Bob. There were phone calls to her boss, letters to the newspaper, even a speech in the Texas legislature up in Austin.

Bob nods sympathetically. "Us Texans," he says. "I guess we never did much care for a little thing like the truth to get in the way of a good story."

He says he's sorry for my mother, that she had to catch all the heat just for trying to unmangle history, and he tells me she seems like a mighty fine woman.

I thank him for that and then mention that I've been talking to Star, though I don't tell him that I hold her hand when I'm with her now, or that the last time I left I kissed her.

"Yes," Bob says. "Yes. That's important. The doctors say we have to keep talking to her, not give it up. They say that might be the only way to pull her out of this, to keep calling her, to keep calling her name, not let her slip in any deeper—"

He pauses, pushes his food with his fork, then says, "You know, Henry, that's the goddamnedest thing here, the way this is working out. The doctors, they have all the technology, all the miracle medicines, everything, but here I am, I feel like I'm standing at my own back door, calling for Star somewheres in the neighborhood playing with the kids when she was little, calling her name, and there's supposed to be something in my voice that makes her know it's *my* voice, and something there that makes her know she has to come in out of the dark, come in for supper or whatever, wash her face and hands and set the table.

"Only now she's hiding someplace in her brain, someplace in her head, but I've got to trust that that same thing will fetch her out. Now what is that thing, Henry?" he asks me. "What the hell do you think that is?"

The correct answer, I could say but don't, is *patterning*, which the physical therapist said means forcing paralyzed limbs through old motions so the muscles don't atrophy, and so a stroke victim's brain can find a way to make those movements automatic again.

It must be the same with voices and sound. I doubt Bob wants to hear that, though, and I don't say anything right away, not until his silence tells me he really does want an answer. Then I give him what I think he wants to hear. I say the word *love*.

Bob's knuckles are white from gripping too hard at the neck of a bottle of Dos Equis, and he seems angry all of a sudden, and all he says back to me is "Maybe."

After dinner I drive to my mother's townhouse, where I've been staying, just outside the interstate loop in a newly developed corner of southwest San Antonio, and I meet a crazy woman who says her name is Tijuana, which I don't believe because she's obviously an Anglo. She lives across the street, and my mother has told me the woman is out every morning and evening in the dark, watering the hard Texas saw grass that grows in patches in front of the apartments. Tijuana catches me getting out of the car and says I should come to a meeting of all the townhouse owners in the complex to talk about the grass. She has called the meeting herself, because she's tired of being the one to work on grass all the time with no help from the developers or anyone else. She says this accusingly, as if I'm to blame.

"I've been watering for two years," she says. "It's too much for one woman alone. Nobody helps. It's their responsibility—the developers. They can sod. Put in a sprinkler system. We have a right to expect this. Me, I can't take it anymore."

The night wind picks up while Tijuana is talking—her voice rising at the end of her sentences in a breathless, almost desperate way, so I can't help believing her—and the temperature drops in the twenty minutes she has me trapped listening to her out by the car. Under the yellow street light I see dust devils spinning out of that brown part of the yard where Tijuana most wants her grass to grow, and where she's watering tonight I see a muddy stream of topsoil running across the sidewalk and into the street.

I excuse myself, finally, and go inside to call my ex-wife, Rennie, in Atlanta. At first I think I'm calling to tell her about my mother's stroke, but after awhile I realize I just want to hear her voice. I want to see if I can catch a hint of what must have been there back when we first met and words were still important. And maybe I want to give her the opportunity to hear some of that in my voice, too—whatever it is between people that Bob has to believe will pull Star out of her coma.

Rennie is sorry, of course, about my mother, but she's also very tired, so we don't talk long. I'm just beginning to tell her about Desgraciado when she muffles the phone and speaks to someone at her end of the line. I ask who she's talking to, but Rennie uses her polite news voice on me. It's opaque and I can't tell a thing.

Later, not able to sleep, I sit in my mother's bedroom and flip through her old issues of *Time* magazine, working my way backward, paying special attention to articles about the hostage who was hanged. In my new chronology, the story of kidnapping, captivity, torture, and death is reversed: the hostage comes back to life; time gradually strips away the layers of suffering; he's reported missing; he's a free man again—his freedom marked only by the absence of his name from the news.

I put down the magazines close to midnight, then turn off the bedroom light, and crouch next to the window to watch Tijuana out on the lawn still watering her saw grass. The silver stream hypnotizes me, arcing away from the hose, dissolving into spray, and I suppose it hypnotizes her, too, like relaxation therapy or meditation. Why else stand there night after night? She knows she'll never be able to grow enough to make any difference—she's washing away all her topsoil, for Christ's sake—so she must be getting something else from it.

Watching Tijuana, I start thinking about Rennie and me when we worked on newspapers right after journalism school, how we both figured if we talked to enough sources, dug through the right documents, shed enough light on enough things, we'd finally get at the truth. Rennie saw a lot of symbolism in my decision to quit writing news for a job on the business side of the paper. She said it was money over integrity. I've tried to explain it to her plenty of times since then—that the truth wasn't doing anything but making me nervous—but she doesn't understand; she still insists I've changed.

I look out the townhouse window again—past midnight now, but I know I'm hours away from sleep—and wonder if this is what my mother sees night after night, the last picture of every long day: Crazy Tijuana across the street in the dark, still watering her saw grass, watering the topsoil, fighting her lonely Texas grass war.

I wake up the next day hung over from dreams, and it's late, almost noon. Bob spent last night on a cot by Star's bed, and I was supposed to relieve him early this morning and sleep there tonight. We had to tell my mother about Desgraciado to explain why we were staying around the clock, but I figured she was strong enough to handle it. I keep telling myself she's getting better and the miracle pit viper venom is working. On the way out the door I pick up the hand mirror she's been asking for and that I've been afraid to give her. My reflection seems haunted—eyes dark, skin sallow, lips dry and white—and the little mirror bends my face at the edges, widens it, distorts it so I can barely recognize my own features.

The heat from the road and the glare from white buildings give me a headache as I drive toward the interstate. When I finally cut on the air-conditioner the shock of the cold leaves me disoriented, and I worry all the way to Medical Center Drive that I may be going in the wrong direction, south instead of north. Once I get to the exit the paperboy sells me a *Light,* but there's no news about the hostage. Already he's been forced off the front page by bigger, more topical stories.

Inside, on the Special Medicine ward, I see three men as soon as I step off the elevator, and I stop cold.

It's Desgraciado, dwarfed between the Hispanic deputy on one side, the Anglo on the other, and they're coming toward me in the hall. Desgraciado wears street clothes, brown suit, no tie, and his hands are manacled in front. His face looks sunken, as if it's been slowly imploding, collapsing in on itself, and he's staring out at me from so far away that I think the next time he closes his eyes he'll have to claw deep into his face to find them again. I feel vulnerable, targeted, and wish I had a weapon so I could strike first, kill Desgraciado before he has a chance to kill me.

He stops and purses his lips.

"This one," he says to the deputies. "*Mi hermano. Mi ángel.* Every day he watches. *Todos días.* Every day he saves my life."

"*Gracias,*" he says to me, and his voice is shattered glass.

The deputies pull Desgraciado around me, and they disappear into the elevator before I can speak. For a long time I stare at the elevator doors, thinking I could still run down the stairs, still catch him on the first floor. I could confront him. I could say some things. Maybe I could even hit him in that vanishing face, make him bleed. Maybe his blood can't clot anymore, and once you get him started bleeding he won't stop until it's all drained out of him, until he's empty, worse than dead, until he's nothing.

I walk slowly to the clerk's desk. She looks up from her Loteria form.

"Please," I say. "The man there, the one with the deputies."

She smiles. "He's gone. He got out—"

"Discharged."

"He won't be back? He's not just gone for tests?"

"No," she says again. "Discharged this morning. Back to his jail."

I thank her, then start to leave.

"Wait," the clerk says. "There." She points behind me.

I don't understand at first, because all I see when I turn is a side hall off the Special Medicine Ward, and at the far end an older couple—the man in jeans, boots, and Western shirt, the woman in a long bathrobe—the two of them engaged in a strange dance, waltzing their way slowly, clumsily up the corridor. But they're not dancing at all, I finally realize. What I see, and what the clerk was pointing at, is my mother moving stiffly, dragging her leg, trying to balance herself, leaning heavily on Star's father's arm.

"Henry," she says, and she lifts her left arm toward me. "Look at me, Henry. I'm walking."

She lets go of Bob to hold on to me, and I expect her to pull me down because of the leaden way she seemed to pull against him, but she turns out to be as light as a child. I could lift her in my arms if I wanted. I could carry her away from all this. Bob's voice reaches me like a faraway echo in the hall. He says my mother's first name—Claire—and says maybe she's done enough for today and he should go for a wheelchair. He slaps me on the back as he heads for the nurses' station.

My mother kisses me. "They came in this morning and said I should try it," she says. "They want to find out how much I can do, and I think I surprised them." Even the side of her face responds when she smiles. "It's wonderful, isn't it, Henry? Don't you think it's wonderful?"

I look at my mother and see that her eyes are rimmed with tears, and I can't remember seeing her this way since I was little. I do think it's wonderful that she's walking. And it's even better because she's safe now that Desgraciado is off the ward, discharged from the hospital, out of our lives. We're all safe now, I tell myself.

Everybody's safe.

Bob is back quickly with the wheelchair. "Now sit right down here, Claire," he says. "You want Henry and me to sneak a couple of beers up here so we can celebrate?"

"Oh Bob," my mother says, and there's something warm in her voice—something in both of their voices—that surprises me.

She rubs her paralyzed hand up and down on my forearm and tells me she's even starting to get feeling back.

"Just a matter of time," Bob says.

He asks my mother if she wants us to bring her back to the room, but she says she'd like to see more of the ward since she's already up. Bob offers to push the chair.

"Aren't you coming, Henry?" my mother asks, but I shake my head. I have to make some calls, I say. My brother and sister will both want to know. And maybe I'll call my father with the news, and maybe Rennie.

They'd like to be together, of course—my mother and Star's father, Claire and Bob—anyone can see that now, even someone who was blind to it before, even me. I walk alone back toward my mother's room at the end of the Special Medicine corridor, but stop at Desgraciado's door, caught by the urge to go in, to search for traces of him. The custodians are already cleaning, though—emptying the garbage, changing the sheets, scouring the floor and the walls, disinfecting everything, and they have surgical masks over their faces, plastic gloves on their hands. There's nothing else to see, no need to look for what's not there. It could have been anybody's room.

I push away from the door and move farther down the corridor, keeping one hand on the wall for balance. The hall seems interminably long this afternoon, but I still have to get to the room at the end. So much has happened today, and I want to be the one to tell Star.

# A Jelly of Light

... and always the moment came when no effort
of thought could prevail against the sensation of
being imbedded in a jelly of light. ... "

—Samuel Beckett, *Murphy*

Cat and that goddamn Bobby—Bud thinks about it all the time. They fool around and then they lie around depressed. That's all they do: fool around and get depressed. Bud would like to fly Cat to Ethiopia for a day. She thinks she's so miserable; he'd show her some real damn misery. And Bobby—Bud has sincerely tried running him off, but Bobby's like all those summer deerflies: he keeps coming back and coming back. Bud has half a mind to kick the boy's ass, but that would only make Cat feel persecuted, and *that* could only make matters worse.

Bud asks his wife, Sunny: What's a boy, nineteen, doing mooning around a girl just turned fifteen? As if Bud himself doesn't really know.

Sunny yawns. She's had narcolepsy for as long as Bud can remember, and he knows tension puts her right to sleep. Fuck it—he's pissed off. "Cat ought to be playing her flute," he says, "not doing it with this guy in the back seat of a two-tone Chevy."

Sunny says something about teenage chakra being naturally low, but that that's no reason for Bud's mind to be in the gutter. Or his mouth either. She yawns again and stretches on the couch. Her eyes are that puffy red they get going into sleep.

Bud says, "Don't go to sleep, Sunny—I want to talk to you about this." But Sunny slips under, and there's no telling how long she'll be gone. Bud thinks about Bobby's pale blue Chevy Impala with the red doors—not the original doors. He says, "That's the kind of car a criminal would drive. We could have him arrested for statutory rape, couldn't we?"

Sunny snores. She's no help. She wouldn't be any help even if she didn't have narcolepsy, because she's been seeking a higher plane of consciousness lately—trying to raise her chakra to another level. And Cat isn't her daughter anyway. Sunny practices SOMA massage—Bud can't remember what the acronym stands for—and when she's not working, she's lotusing on a rice mat in the bedroom, trying to hit that higher chakra. Bud has forgotten if there are supposed to be eight chakra levels or nine. Sunny thinks she's at about six now—she says that and points to her head: sixth chakra. Bud figures he must be a minus-something chakra. He also suspects Sunny might be making a little extra money giving her SOMA customers what they call a "hand release." He hasn't asked her about it, though, because he's not sure he wants to know.

Bud pinches Sunny's nose until she quits snoring. She doesn't wake up. He's got enough on his mind already without having to worry about her. And hell, even if he did ask her if she was giving tugs, she'd fall asleep too fast for him to get anywhere with it anyway.

So Bud's still thinking about Cat and that goddamn Bobby. He figures they're doing it right there in the house in the afternoon after Cat gets out of school. When Bud and Sunny are working. He's never caught them at it. Wherever the hell else they do it, Bud has no idea, and he's not sure he wants to know that either. As it is, he wishes he'd never asked half the damn questions he's recently gotten answers for.

"What the hell's wrong with them?" he'd been asking Sunny. That was a few weeks ago. "What are they so depressed for? Don't they have anything to do?" There was Cat on the phone—sighing; talking in whispers like she had anything to her life worth keeping secret. There were Cat and Bobby, sitting on the sofa holding hands and watching MTV and not smiling, not moving, not saying a word. "Are they doing drugs?" Bud had asked Sunny. Sunny said she doubted it.

"Then what?" Bud wanted to know. Tina Turner was on the TV, wearing a tight sequined jean jacket and singing a song called "What's Love Got to Do with It." Sunny's mouth moved with the words.

"You know," Bud said when he got no response, "I read that Ike used to beat Tina up. You'd think she could clean up on Ike if she wanted." Tina also wore high heels and a tight black leather miniskirt.

Sunny said she read that Tina was a Buddhist, and she practiced Zen meditation—that was how she got over Ike.

"Yeah," Bud said. "Well I heard that Ike and Sonny Bono and all those other ex-husband washouts were going to get together and start their own band."

Later, Sunny told Bud what Cat had told Sunny that Cat and Bobby had been doing that under no circumstances was Bud supposed to know about. Sunny also told Bud that she thought Cat and Bobby wanted to get married, or at least live together, but knew there were obstacles—like their ages, like money, like a place to live, like Bud.

Bud just sat there.

"They're second chakra, Bud," Sunny said. "They can't help it."

"Meaning what?" Bud was thinking about his little Cat, not too long after Bud's first wife left them. Cat out on a tumbling mat with forty other kids in leotards. How surprised he'd been when little Cat, red hair flying, ran hard, touched the springboard, flew over six other little bodies curled up like barrels, landed and rolled her way into a handspring, then ended in a split.

"Meaning," Sunny said, "that their spirituality is defined by their eroticism."

As it turned out, Cat had been having sex since almost a year ago when she was still fourteen, had in fact been screwing Bobby since she was fourteen and a freshman and he was eighteen and a senior. When Bud found that out he took off right away looking for Bobby and Cat, thinking he was going to have to kill somebody.

He still wants to kill Bobby when he thinks too much about

it. Sometimes when Bud sees the two of them—on the couch, depressed, watching MTV, or walking in from a date, as silent as if somebody'd just died—the thoughts make him a little crazy: what Cat and Bobby might have just been doing; what Cat and Bobby are going to be doing when they're alone.

That's when Bud leaves the house. It's spring and the yellow flies attack his face, clog themselves up in his hair. He doesn't bother to slap them anymore. Kill one and three more take its place. Bud drives his truck up to Georgia. Somehow he thinks they wouldn't be having these problems if they'd never moved down from Georgia in the first place, even if it is just over the state line. He thinks: Fuck Florida. Florida looks like a gun to Bud. A loaded gun. Bud lives in the handle, but feels like the thing's pointed right at his head.

After an hour, Bud takes a right off 319 to the asphalt entrance road for the Thomasville-Moultrie Municipal Airport. He remembers when that road was still red clay, packed as hard as any runway. Hell, Bud remembers when the landing strip at Thom-Moultrie was a turned-under peanut field.

Bud has a little Cessna 140, in the last hangar out, which he built from a crate of parts he bought at a sheriff's auction two years ago. Most of the planes—the Pipers and Cessnas and Beech-crafts—are lined up beside the runway, wings pinned down with steel wire. From the air it looks like a giant bug collection. Bud got the hangar because he's acting manager of the airport. That means Henry Kirbo, the manager, is in detox again. Bud works on engines, handles preflight servicing, stamps flight plans, and refuses to give flying lessons anymore. But he doesn't think about any of that when he's thinking about Cat. He drives straight to the hangar. Pulls back the big doors, which always grind because the rollers need oil. Primes the fuel line. Test-flaps his wings and tail. Checks the wind sock.

He's been known to go up in the rain.

Bud blocks the television. Cat and Bobby look up at him, though not exactly surprised. Bud doesn't know if they work on it—not showing any emotion, like it's the thing to do—or if they honest-to-god don't have any emotions.

"Cat," he says. "Go help Sunny in the kitchen."

Cat sighs and whispers "god!" under her breath, only she's particularly hard on the *g* and it comes out "cod!" She gets up slowly, as if she's struggling against gravity. She's almost as tall as Cassandra, her mother, Bud notices, though she doesn't have any breasts to speak of. She looks a lot like Cassandra.

Cat sniffs. "Cod! She's cooking tofu, Daddy. I hate tofu."

Cat goes anyway. Bud looks down at Bobby, who doesn't look back. The song on the MTV sounds like Creedence Clearwater Revival, which surprises Bud because he hasn't heard them in years.

"You're not in school," he says to Bobby.

Bobby works hard to look bored; Bud remembers when he was that way around adults. "I graduated," Bobby says, as if it's one of his great failures in life.

"And what the hell do you do when you're not hanging around

my daughter?" Bud doesn't want to sound this harsh, but he can't help it.

Bobby looks up at this. He's got a fifteen dollar haircut that Bud figures he could improve on for free—blindfolded, with dull scissors. "I work for my dad."

"Doing what?"

"He's a lawyer."

"What does that make you—a junior partner?" Bud knows he's being sarcastic, but Jesus, how's he supposed to talk to this little jerk?

"I sweep."

"You sweep?"

"And I mow the lawn."

Bud is sure that's Creedence on the MTV, but he's damned if he can place the song. It's definitely John Fogerty's voice.

Bud turns around to look. Sure enough, John Fogerty is standing in the middle of a street, playing his electric guitar. Bud remembers the song now. He's heard it a couple of times on the radio: "The Old Man Is Down the Road." He remembers a story his brother told him once about how Creedence couldn't afford microphones when they first started out, and John Fogerty sang without one—over the amplifiers. Bud bets nobody has to shout like that anymore, and he wonders whatever happened to the rest of Creedence. He used to love that band: "Green River," "Proud Mary, "Bad Moon Rising."

"Listen here," he says to Bobby. "Cat loves to fly in airplanes. Have you ever been up?"

"Up. You mean up in airplanes?"

"Of course."

"No sir." Bud hadn't expected to be called "sir." It throws him a little.

"Tomorrow you tell your daddy the lawyer that Cat's daddy is taking you to Georgia to fly in an airplane, and can he please excuse you from sweeping the floor for one afternoon."

Bobby just looks at Bud, but he doesn't say anything. Bud knows the boy will come all the same. He also knows that tomorrow he's going to make Bobby wish he'd never met Cat, or Cat's daddy, and sure as hell not Cat's daddy's airplane.

That night Bud rolls on top of Sunny while she sleeps. It's the narcolepsy: she never wakes up. She told him when they first got together to go ahead and do it to her if he wanted. Bud does, but he gets discouraged. With Sunny so inert, it's only slightly better than masturbating. He's tried getting Sunny to make love when she's awake, but she always falls asleep when she gets excited and it never works out. She says it's no big deal—she's past that chakra anyway.

Bud stares at her in the dark. She really is pretty. And she really has been good for him, even if she's not everything he always expected of a woman. Bud turns on his back and studies the water spot on the ceiling that he's been meaning to fix for about three months. Hell, he's probably not everything she always expected of a man, either.

Bud closes his eyes and thinks about Cat's mother. Cassandra lives in Atlanta, and they haven't seen her in over a year. Bud thinks maybe if he can figure out Cassandra he'll understand Cat a little better, but he won't bet the plane on it.

Bud and Cassandra had been married seven years when Cassandra told him their sex was lousy.

"I have never been able to get off without my vibrator," she told him.

Bud was stunned. He'd always thought they had a great sex life. He'd prided himself, in fact, on his performance in bed. It wasn't something he'd ever brag about, but he never came too quickly. He'd never been impotent.

"I didn't even know you *had* a vibrator," he said.

"Well maybe that's part of the problem, Bud. You don't notice what you ought to be noticing."

Bud couldn't believe it. How he could have been thinking one thing for so damn long, when it was another thing altogether that was true.

"You never?" he asked her, incredulous.

"Not without my vibrator."

Bud knew right then they were finished. He didn't want it to be true, but it was. When that one thing came out into the open, it was like everything else was bound to follow—couldn't help but follow. The mean truth has a force all its own, and once it gets a little momentum going, God help anybody who stands in the way. Bud was crushed.

Cassandra tried hard to work things out, but Bud was unresponsive. She suggested Bud hold the vibrator when they were in bed; he started sleeping on the couch. She signed them up for a sexual sensitivity seminar; he told her to go by herself. She started seeing a doctor; Bud said he was keeping Cat no matter what.

Bud was a real bastard when it came down to divorce: he kept Cat; he got everything. Cassandra married the doctor. Bud assumed the guy, being a doctor, must know plenty about anatomy that would make him the lover Bud apparently wasn't. He probably brought Cassandra to screaming, clawing, bed-breaking orgasms with a flick of this, a turn of that, a twist, a screw. The thought of it drove Bud nuts. He stopped eating. He stopped talking to people unless he absolutely had to.

He even pulled Cat out of school for a couple of months. He'd sit her beside him at the airport, whatever he was working on. She'd hand him tools. Fill buckets. File flight plans. Clear blocks. Cat didn't say much either, and Bud never knew if she felt as bad as he did—which is what he hoped—or if his silence was too formidable for her. Late in the day they would get a plane and go flying. Usually south—out of Georgia, over Florida. At the coast they would run parallel to the beach for a while, maybe scare a few gulls, then fly home.

One night Bud saw Cassandra and her new husband driving out to a movie. He drove over to their house and broke in, though at first he didn't know why. He stood in the living room looking for something to steal—thinking anybody who broke into a house has to steal something. The place smelled of Cassandra, though there didn't seem to be any visible signs of her. The living room was more like a doctor's waiting room: old copies of *Field & Stream* on the coffee table, *People* magazine, even a handful of pamphlets on high cholesterol and obesity.

Bud went into the bedroom and immediately thought Holiday

Inn. Dull prints on the wall. Dull spread on the bed. Dull panel-
ing on the chest of drawers. And a vibrator on the bedside stand.
Bud picked it up. It looked like one of those blow-dryers for hair.
It looked like a gun. A lot of things looked like guns to Bud. He
gripped the handle, pointed the round knob at his temple, and
fired. It vibrated his whole head. Bud turned it off. Put it back on
the stand. Went home and sent Cat back to school the next day.

Later, Cassandra and her doctor husband moved to Atlanta.
Bud and Cat moved to Florida, and Bud met Sunny.

When Bud and Bobby take off, Bud deliberately hangs long on the
runway before dropping the flaps. It looks as if they might hit the
pine stand two hundred yards off the end of the tarmac, but Bud
knows they'll clear by a good thirty feet.

"Fuck me! You could of hit those trees!" Bobby yells before he
can catch himself.

Bud figures everything's going according to plan, and he eases
off the throttle, causing them to dip—just enough to make Bobby's
stomach lurch, like a sudden elevator descent. On the drive up, Bud
gave Bobby a couple of beers so he'd be primed for the flight. Bud
himself never flies when he's been drinking. He pretended to drink
a beer himself and poured out half when Bobby wasn't looking.

Already Bobby is sweating it. The armpits of his Duran Duran T-
shirt are wet, and the cockpit's beginning to stink. Bud knows the
signs. He banks hard left and holds to turn a full 180, and suddenly
they're in the sun. Bud's got shades; Bobby throws his hands up in
front of his face.

"Fuck me, man. Can't see."

Bud levels out. "Down there's where you just took off from."

Bobby looks down and looks back up quickly. The first time up in a small plane, Bud knows, is like what you always thought jumping off the top of the Empire State Building must be like. A long ways down . . . too much time to think . . . no question about what's going to happen when you hit. Nobody trusts a small plane. It's nothing like a jetliner—fucking sky bus. Bud doesn't know what flying's like exactly: it's like nothing at all; it's like what you always wished life was when you were a kid, and finally you have it, it's yours, and you hardly know what to do with it, it's so god- damn great.

Cat used to love flying with Bud. Hell, if her legs had been longer she could have flown by herself. He'd sit her in his lap, take her through the controls, give her the wheel, and they'd fly together—Bud talking softly in her ear and working the flap ped- als on the floor. There was always a crack in the window, and air would scream through, blowing Cat's red hair into Bud's face. It almost seemed he could taste that hair: sweet, like cotton candy when it's just been spun onto the stick. They were always bor- rowing planes and renting planes, trading work for planes. When Bud found his Cessna in a crate and figured he could afford it, he thought he'd be teaching Cat to fly by herself. That gave him a real kick: thinking about Cat flying solo. Like she had enough of him in her that he could trust she would always—always what? Bud has to think about that.

Always just love him, he guesses.

But Cat lost interest. Cat started playing the flute. Cat discovered boys. Started having sex. Started having sex with Bobby.

"Hang on," Bud says, grinding his teeth. "We're gonna roll."

"What?"

Bud raises an aileron, lowers another, pushes them through a couple of barrel rolls. Bobby goes white. His mouth drops. When Bud rights the Cessna, Bobby heaves, and Bud slaps a hand over the boy's mouth: "Don't you throw up in here! Don't do it."

Bobby's eyes are wide. He flails around, trying to grab something to puke in. Nothing. There's nothing. Bud keeps his hand clamped onto Bobby's face: "Don't do it," he says, but Bobby heaves again.

"Swallow it!" Bud yells. "You swallow it." There's too much violence in Bud's voice. Bobby swallows, gags, swallows again. His face is beaded with sweat. Bud almost feels sorry for him—but not too sorry. He tilts the wheel back and they climb about five hundred feet into the sun.

"What do you say?" Bud asks. His smile is almost evil. "Want to try it again?"

They fly north, following Interstate 75 toward Atlanta a little way above Tifton, and that makes Bud think about Cassandra. Cassandra hated flying.

Bobby complains that he's got a headache. "Man, I don't know about this—"

Bud cuts the engine and doesn't pull them out of the downward drift until they can read the STUCKEY'S PECAN ROLL signs by the highway. Bobby's really stinking up the cockpit, and Bud can't stop thinking about Cassandra. He doesn't want to think about her, but he can't help it. It's the price he pays for what he's doing to Cat's boyfriend.

They fly for an hour, Bud turning every wild trick he knows into a nightmare for Bobby, who starts to look a little green. Finally Bud banks sharply, flopping Bobby against the door, as they circle back over the Thom-Moultrie Airport. Bobby tried puking once more during the flight, and Bud made him swallow it that time, too. Bud figures there's no way he can avoid going to hell for that.

Francine in the tower says it's all right for Bud to land, and he noses the Cessna in. He considers taking a few hard bounces when he touches, but he looks over at Bobby, slumped against his shoulder belt, and decides it's not worth risking a bent axle. Bud greases the landing and angles clean off the runway in front of his hangar. He cuts the engine, leans back as the propeller coughs around, and only then realizes how tired he is. Bud sees his knuckles are white from holding the wheel too hard. He shakes himself: he knows it's just the heat from the engine.

Bobby fumbles at the door, and Bud leans over to unlock it. "Flight a little rough for you?" he asks, but without much feeling. Only a sick man enjoys seeing other people suffer, even if he is the cause.

Bobby doesn't answer. He falls out the door face down and throws up in the oily grass.

The drive home is quiet. Bud makes Bobby ride in the back of the truck because he smells so bad. Bobby lies down on a canvas tarp, and he's asleep when Bud drops him off at his parents' house. Bud wonders what a nineteen-year-old is doing still living at home, but mostly he's just glad to be rid of Bobby, who wobbles across the trim lawn toward the white double-doors. Bud is disgusted with the kid for putting up with Bud's shit all day.

Bud's house is six miles east of town, up a rutted dirt road. Oaks form a dark canopy at dusk, and Bud drives with his headlights on down what seems like a long, twisting tunnel to somewhere underground. It doesn't feel like going home.

Candlelight sputters in the window of an upstairs room— Sunny and Bud's bedroom. That usually means Sunny's on her rice mat meditating. Bud wonders how Sunny knows when she rises another chakra. She seems pretty sure of it, doesn't ever question what she's doing. He has asked her before exactly what it is she's trying to get at, and she says it's hard to put into words: "I guess you might say I want to be above everything but not be snooty about it. Above everything, including myself."

What Bud thinks this means is that when Sunny reaches her top chakra there will no longer be any consequences to her actions, because Sunny and What-Sunny-Does will be two totally different things. It's a sophisticated idea for him, and when he asks her if that's right, Sunny says, "Sort of. But not entirely." Bud leaves it alone.

As he approaches the house, he hears flute music. At first he thinks MTV, but then he realizes it's Cat playing her flute—something she hasn't done in months, since she quit the school band. Bud feels smug for a minute, like maybe he's responsible. The whole day seems right. But then Bud recognizes the song—that

Tina Turner song—and he understands that she's just fooling around, trying to figure out the arrangement.

He sneaks inside the house and unplugs the phone. At least Bobby's not around. And if tonight Cat's playing stuff she heard on the MTV, she might be back to the school band stuff tomorrow. Bud peeks into Cat's room—the door's partly open. She's sitting cross-legged on her bed, naked except for her panties. She doesn't see him. Bud steps back quickly, embarrassed.

Cat. Naked.

Bud backtracks down the hall. He doesn't know why he's tip-toeing around his own house, but he doesn't want to stop either. He goes upstairs. Sunny's eyes are closed, and she's chanting softly when Bud enters the bedroom. He stops just inside the door. Sunny's wearing a robe, and she's in her lotus position—back straight, legs crossed, hands on her knees.

She says "Om," and she holds the note until her breath runs out. She says "Om" again. Bud knew a guy once who did transcendental meditation. Bud won the guy's secret mantra in a poker game. Bud tried it out, but it didn't work for him. Sunny says she doesn't need a mantra. Mantras are just crutches anyway. Om suits her fine.

Bud watches Sunny for a long time. Usually he's happy for her to be meditating. She seems to get something out of it, even if Bud doesn't quite understand what. Tonight, though, Bud wishes she would stop. He wishes he could make her stop. Maybe they could talk about Cat for a while. Maybe they could make love, and just for once she would stay awake. At least give him the attention her massage customers get when she maybe sells them sterile hand jobs.

He's learned some things; Bud thinks he can be sensitive now to a woman's needs. Sunny hums another "Om."

Bud closes his eyes, frustrated, and sees Sunny climbing her chakras one at a time, like Jacob's ladder to the clouds, and he sees himself stuck at the bottom, losing her as she rises up and up beyond him into the ozone, and heaven, and the stars, and black holes, and quarks, and quasars, and whatever the fuck else is up there. Bud sees himself chasing her; he gets out the old Cessna— he can fly too, goddamnit. But it's no good. Sunny is gone on her chakras. Cat drives away in some boy's Chevy. Bud sees himself circling the airport. Circling and circling, brushing clouds, not wanting to land.

# Painting the Baby's Room

My wife let her blood sugar get low last week and she fainted. One minute she was standing at the door talking to the police officer about the thefts, and the next minute she was on the floor, the cop offering her water and saying something like, "Oh my god, you could have fallen down the stairs." Judy got an egg lump on the back of her head, and since she's six months pregnant, the doctor told her to go to bed and stay there for a while. The police officer left his nightstick at our house.

Judy didn't want to go to bed; she thinks she sleeps too much anyway, and she'd been planning to paint the baby's room. She agreed only when I said I'd take a few days off from work and paint the baby's room myself. The doctor had told me privately that someone should watch her for a few days because the fall was harder than he'd let on, and because you had to be careful with head injuries, and because there was always the chance that the fall might bring on early labor. There didn't seem to be much else I could do, even though we need the money. I've been substitute teaching a ninth-grade algebra class for the past three months, and when a substitute teacher doesn't work, he doesn't get paid.

The next day first thing I headed out the door to buy paint. Judy had told me babies have webbed feet when they're just starting to form as embryos, so I thought about ours being a swimmer. I knew Judy wanted yellow—her room when she was a kid was always yellow—but I decided to surprise her with the swimmer motif and so bought a couple of gallons of aquamarine latex instead. And a roller and a pan and a small brush for trim.

Back home I went into the garage and knew right away something was missing, though it was a few minutes before I could figure out what. My barbells had been rolled off the mat I have down there. What was missing turned out to be an old lamp with a Niagara Falls shade—the kind that turns so it looks like the water's really moving. It didn't work anymore, but I was still mad. Especially since Judy had just called the police the day before about the thefts. Our house is actually a garage apartment, so whoever stole that lamp did it right under our bed, just a couple of feet and a floor from where we were sleeping. I put fifty pounds on the bar and did some fast curls, thinking about that nightstick upstairs, and the skull of the thief, and the egg lump on Judy's head.

We're not in a very good location. We live a couple of blocks from the bus station, and our street attracts people shuffling between there and that part of town they call Beat Street. The problem with the garage is it doesn't have a door. It's where we store stuff, since there isn't room upstairs. Junk mostly. Like busted lamps. And some books. Old clothes, a few tools, rusty bicycles, mirrors, chairs with three legs. I had hung a green tarp from the Army/Navy Store over the entrance for a little privacy when we first moved in a couple of years ago, but that obviously hadn't stopped anybody from entering, at least not at night. They'd stolen a Monopoly board with all the paper money, a pair of needle-nosed pliers, a set of Allen wrenches, an old black-and-white TV with no horizontal hold—all that over the past couple of weeks—and, worst of all, Judy's mother's old black Singer machine. I'd been planning to get it fixed. They also keyed the side of our old Datsun, which we parked next to the garage, but that car was so beat up already I almost didn't notice, and if they'd stolen it I wouldn't have cared.

I curled the fifty until I broke out in a sweat, and then went upstairs with the paint. Judy was in bed surrounded by baby books, although she had told me that since she fell and got the egg lump she could read only a few minutes before she got a headache.

"Look at this picture," Judy said, holding up one of the books. "Peter, look." On the cover was a tiny, red, eyeless humanoid partly shrouded in a filmy gauze, its thumb tucked under its upper lip. The creature was curled up and bound by a tight-fitting, transparent sack.

"That's our baby," Judy said.

I shivered with claustrophobia.

The aquamarine seemed a lot darker poured into the pan, and as soon as I hit the wall with the roller, I knew I'd made a mistake. It never looks the same in real life as the paint samples at the store. Because I'd already bought the paint, though, I thought I had to use it.

For a couple of hours I pushed the roller, the blue-green sucking to the walls and speckling me and the drop cloth, and the room grew darker with each roll, like storm clouds gathering and blocking the sun.

My tongue started hurting, and the more I painted that depressing aquamarine, and the more I thought about the garage thefts, the more it hurt. Judy says it's anxiety. She says when you worry too much your body produces acid that makes your tongue sore. I think it was from too much spicy Mexican food, but I'm a math teacher, not a doctor.

I stopped painting when my tongue started throbbing. In the kitchen I poured a full glass of ice water, and for five minutes stuck my tongue in it until the stinging cold turned into a general numbness.

When I finished the room it was with about as much satisfaction as convicts must feel after breaking up rocks with sledgehammers. I knew as soon as I painted the last inch of trim that a child would probably rather not be born than live in a room that ugly. Especially after nine claustrophobic months underwater locked inside a tight Baggie. A baby needs something light and airy, a room to breathe in.

Judy smiled at me in our bedroom after I'd cleaned up. "Listen to this, Peter." She read from one of her books: "'By about six months your baby has grown to approximately a foot in length and weighs around one and a half pounds. Her eyes open and she moves about in a quart of amniotic fluid.' A quart? I always thought it must be gallons." She laughed and laid her hands on her belly. "It feels like gallons."

I shut the door tight on the aquamarine room and made Judy

promise she wouldn't go in. The next morning I was back at the store early, loading up on Sears' standard white latex. The saleslady nodded approvingly as she rang up the purchase.

Everything seemed all right in the garage when I got back home. I did a dozen clean and jerks with 150 pounds on the bar, then knocked off 100 and curled with the 50 that were left. I had bought the free weights five months before at a yard sale—a bar and 200 pounds of weights. What happened was we'd just found out Judy was pregnant, and we were babysitting my brother's little girl, Annie, who was one and a half. Annie cried almost the entire evening. Judy and I had taken turns holding her, walking with her from room to room, but I had never known babies could get so heavy. My arms were Jell-O. So I bought the weights to build up some strength, figuring I needed thick tree limbs for holding my own baby, Arnold Schwarzenegger arms for those long, colicky nights that were sure to come.

Since I hadn't painted the ceiling of the baby's room before, I hadn't bothered to scrape it down and wash it as I had done for the walls. Old paint curled up in places like dried leaves over my head, just waiting to drop into a crib or into a baby's mouth, so I spent the morning standing on a chair chipping away loose paint and berating myself for being so careless, for not seeing it before. Twice I had to stop and soak my tongue in ice water. I guess the pressure of things was starting to get to me. Substitute teaching doesn't pay much even when I do work; I've been hoping to land a full-time position in the fall, but nothing's certain. Judy teaches piano lessons on other people's pianos, but even our combined income is low. The garage thefts—I would have laughed those off before Judy got pregnant, but now—

Even the little things were worrying me. Judy had told me a couple of months ago that the fetus can hear really well because sound travels better through the water around the child than it does through air. She said some doctors say people's personalities are affected by what they hear during the pregnancy, and she read me a story about a symphony conductor whose mother played a lot of Mozart while he was in the womb. So every chance I got for awhile I was playing old rock-and-roll records—Chuck Berry, Little Richard, Jerry Lee Lewis—because there's no way of knowing if rock and roll will still be around when the kid's old enough to appreciate it.

"Hey, Peter," Judy called from the other room. "Listen to this—this is scary: 'The most amazing development during the last few months is the staggeringly complex process of brain maturation. It is at this time that the higher functions of the brain begin to appear. Research has shown conclusively that proper diet during the last few weeks of pregnancy is essential. Under-nutrition during this time can result in a baby who is severely mentally retarded, even though not of low birth weight.'"

There was a silence from the bedroom, and I waited. Usually things like that shook Judy up. They shook me up. I expected to hear her crying, which would be my signal to climb down off my chair to go hold her. We stopped getting the newspaper three months ago because the headlines were upsetting her too much.

I was already heading for our room, ready to be the consoling husband, when she snorted and said maybe I ought to run out for a couple of Big Macs.

"Antiretardation food," she said, and then she laughed, and I heard her sigh and flip through a couple of pages.

But I didn't laugh. In that minute I was angry and disgusted, instead: angry with her for being pregnant, disgusted with myself for being a part of this thing that I had no control over. It was the same feeling I used to get on carnival rides at county fairs: trapped by my own passivity or stupidity, at the mercy of rusted tracks and gears and steel and speed and some minimum-wage snuff-dipper in a greasy baseball cap, no excitement for me there, just doom. That was no baby inside Judy, waiting to be born. That was me.

I pushed open the door, frustrated. "I don't think that's funny, Judy," I said, my voice hard. "What if something happened? Something like that? What if something happened to the baby?"

I caught myself. Of course she'd just been kidding, and I knew that, but now I could see that I'd hurt her feelings. She wasn't crying, but her face said it all: the hard lines of surprise, the wounded set of her eyes. "I'm sorry. I'm sorry," I said quickly.

My tongue hurt worse than ever, but I deserved to suffer. I went downstairs and lay down on the mat in the garage, the barbell sitting on my chest with 180 pounds, and I pressed weights for twenty minutes, my tongue throbbing the whole time.

It was eight o'clock that night before I finished painting the baby's room, and I was almost too tired to care that the aquamarine showed through. It was going to take another coat the next day, which meant another couple of gallons of paint. I'd thought it over, though, and decided the second coat would have to be enamel. Enamel's more expensive, but it's thicker, less likely to peel, and you can wash it when a baby smears food on it. If I skipped a few school lunches the money would balance out.

I had a hard time sleeping that night. Judy must have gotten up half a dozen times to go to the bathroom, and I never failed to wake up with her, jarred out of nervous dreams. Once I lay there in a stupor for probably five minutes before I realized Judy hadn't left the bed at all. She was still sleeping beside me, curled up on her side surrounded by pillows. She looked as if she were in a big nest, and she looked so peaceful, all those muscles in her face relaxed, her features softened. I almost believed I could reach over and press my thumb along certain lines like a sculptor and change her looks. Widen that mouth and raise those brows and she'd be Sophia Loren. Push those cheek bones higher and she'd be Katharine Hepburn. I saw a way to make her Bette Davis, but I never have much liked Bette Davis.

I got out of bed without really thinking why at first. At the apartment door I found the policeman's nightstick, and I brought it with me down the stairs and under the canvas flap into the garage. Enough yellow light from a street lamp filtered through the small window on the side so that I could make out the shapes of our possessions. Against the back wall, wrapped in hefty garbage bags, were a dozen boxes of books—cheap paperbacks, old college texts, stuff we'd never read again. But I don't know how to throw away a book. There were books in those boxes given to me when I was a child; I thought maybe I'd drag them out again when our kid was old enough. They'd probably seem dated these days, though—stories about brave fire fighters and loyal dogs and Doctor Dan the Band-Aid Man. Judy showed me a catalog once of modern children's books. It seemed as if half of them were supposed to help kids cope with divorce or death or new schools.

I sat down in an old overstuffed chair and tapped my palm with the nightstick. My father told me once that he and my mother used to sit with me after supper out on the front steps of our little house. That was during the baby boom, so the people on either side had infants, too, and they would all park on their stoops at dusk to talk with the neighbors and play with the kids. The only problem was teenagers who used to speed up and down the neighborhood streets. My father bought a little red wagon for pulling me around in, and he used to line that wagon up on the sidewalk facing the street. When a speedster made the mistake of roaring up our road at dusk, my father just gave that wagon a little kick and sent it rolling down the sidewalk and into the street.

I doubt my father ever sat up with a nightstick in a dark garage at three A.M. on the chance of catching a burglar, though. After half an hour I went back upstairs to soak my tongue in ice water and go back to bed, and it was almost noon the next day before I woke up. Judy had fixed her own cheese toast and juice, and she was stretched out on the lumpy living room sofa doing a nutrition chart.

At Sears that day, the same saleslady rang up my purchase. She looked concerned as she priced the enamel, and I felt like explaining that everything was under control, that this would be the last coat, that I wouldn't be spending any more money, but then I remembered I was going to brush-paint the whole room, not just the trim, so I had to go back for a larger brush.

Judy was up when I got home, and she wanted to help me finish the baby's room. Her head, she said, was fine—no more headaches—and she was tired of lying around the house doing nothing. I said "no" like a parent, which annoyed her, and it looked for a moment as if we were going to argue. I should have known better. That was how the birthing class teacher had talked to Judy, which was also why we had quit the class. The teacher, a certified Bradley instructor, had been criticizing the breathing techniques of Lamaze, and Judy had argued with the woman, saying Lamaze had its merits and seemed to work fine for a lot of women.

"Ah, sister," the woman had smiled, closing her eyes, "once you've had your Bradley child you'll understand."

"I'm not your sister," Judy had said so only I could hear, and when that class ended we never went back. That's when Judy started buying books on different birthing methods, books on nutrition and breastfeeding, books on pregnancy, books on taking care of infants. She'd been disengaging herself from everything for awhile—from her piano students, from newspapers, from friends who talked about themselves—and dropping out of the birthing class seemed like one more step in that retreat.

So I backed down on painting the baby's room when Judy offered a compromise: she would do the trim, then go back to bed. I would paint the walls and the ceiling, although she thought I was being foolish not using a roller. She didn't say a word about the smudges of aquamarine still visible at the edges of the new coat of white, which I appreciated. I put an old Rolling Stones album on the record player—*Beggar's Banquet*—and we painted together most of the afternoon. She knew what I was up to with my rock and roll, and she put on a record of her own after each of mine—Tony Bennett, Nat King Cole, Andy Williams: records Judy's mother had taught her to sing by.

After we finished and I cleaned the brushes and tossed out the empty cans, I drove to the grocery store and bought a couple of steaks for dinner. It meant no school lunches for a week, but what the hell. And to top it off *The Sons of Katie Elder* was on television that night. Dean Martin was in it, but John Wayne made up for that. Judy fell asleep halfway through, but I stayed up until the end, though I'd seen it before when I was a kid. *Katie Elder* was one of my father's favorites.

The room seemed suddenly very empty when I switched off the set, though, and I thought about turning it back on to watch the news. Judy lay on her side near the edge of the bed facing the wall, her back to me. The shades were drawn, and the room was even darker than it needed to be. I didn't hear any cars outside or any loud stereos bothering the neighborhood. The baby's room was painted, we'd had our steak, the movie was over.

Judy turned away from the wall. "Peter."

"Yeah?"

She was crying, and I put my arm around her, cradling her head. "I'm scared," she said. "What if the baby doesn't like us? What if I don't like the baby? What if something happens?"

I pushed away some hair that had fallen in her face.

"I read all these books and I read them and I just don't know—" She was still crying. "I don't even know if it's a boy or a girl, and it's going to change everything. It could be a devil. I don't even know this person."

I laughed. "We're not going to have a little devil," I said. "Hey—" I pulled Judy closer. "A little devil—" I liked the sound of the words, the way those soft consonants rolled off my tongue. "A little devil?"

Judy laughed too. "Don't make fun of me," she said, but she didn't mean it.

"A little devil," I said. "We're not going to have a little devil." I kissed her on the mouth, but couldn't hold the kiss very long; my tongue started hurting. Judy relaxed, and I told her what she wanted to hear—that the baby would be fine, that everything would work out okay—and soon her breathing turned deep and regular with that edge of a snore that let me know she was sleeping again.

But I was wide awake.

My tongue started throbbing, as if it were swollen too large for my mouth, as if my teeth were cutting into the sides, and I pulled my arm carefully out from under Judy's head and went into the kitchen. A few minutes later I pressed my mouth over the top of the water glass, and the ice cubes crowded around my tongue. Every time I exhaled a white cloud rose around my face in the dark, like cool winter breath.

I'd probably been sitting there for ten minutes when I heard the noise. It came from downstairs in the garage.

I grabbed the policeman's nightstick; my fingers locked naturally around the grip as if I'd been carrying it all my life, and the hard plastic casing felt cool in my palm. I opened the door soundlessly and slipped out onto the top step. The stairs run down the side of our house, and I'd have to get all the way to the bottom before I could see into the garage. Like a burglar myself, I descended, holding the rail and cross-stepping down.

Five steps from the bottom I stopped. For thirty seconds I held my breath, but couldn't hear a thing. Just the buzz of the quiet night, a car shifting gears a few streets over. Nothing from the garage. Pressing my ear against the wall I strained to pick up some new noise, but I couldn't be sure of anything. I started to doubt whether there had been a noise in the first place.

Stopping to listen also made me stop to think, and as I leaned against the side of the house, I wondered if I really planned to smack someone with the policeman's club, which no longer felt so cool in my hand. What was he going to steal? The lawn mower? It was the landlord's. Our books? I'd already read them. What if somebody cleaned out the entire garage? It wouldn't be that great a loss. More space for more junk.

And what about protecting the family? What did I think I was going to do, march downstairs and make the world safe for children? It didn't matter what I did, or who I found in the garage, or what he was stealing. My kid, our kid, was still going to have to grow up in an imperfect world, make his own way down that treacherous path of drug dealers and perverts, people who steal things and hurt things and think nothing of it. My tongue was hurting again, and two cars squealed tires a few blocks over. I couldn't shelter our kid from divorce or death or schools or sex or broken hearts or people who hate themselves so they think they have to hate you, too. He was still going to have to figure out a way to make a dollar for himself and be fair to other people at the same time. How to get along with bosses he didn't like. What to do about God.

And what if I did find a thief down there robbing our garage? Nothing I could do about that was going to guarantee our kid would like me, or Judy, or even—how could I even think this?—that we would like the kid.

And then I heard another noise in the garage, and there was no mistaking this one. It was the sound of a twenty-pound free weight slipping off a bar and dropping onto the floor. He was stealing my barbells.

In less time than it took to think about it, I was down the steps and flinging open the tarp in the doorway. A surprised thief looked up at me—he was still holding the bar with weights on one end— and I said, "Son of a bitch," and slapped him hard on the side of the head with the nightstick. That was the sound it made—a slap—and he went down like meat.

I thought he was dead at first, but he had a pulse. There was no getting around the bruised face and the rising lump, but I didn't see any blood. I studied his face and decided he looked a little like me. Not much. A little shorter. A little younger. Hair a little longer. I used to wear my hair long.

Judy and I sat up for a long time after they took the man away. She listened while I babbled about what had happened, about how it was all over so quickly that I couldn't remember a thing. Each time I told the story, though, I remembered a little more, until even I thought I was making some of it up. She made me talk to her belly and tell it to the baby. As it turned out our thief stayed in the hospital for three days with a concussion, but mostly just for observation. One officer told me all they'd be able to charge him with was criminal trespass, since he hadn't actually taken anything, and there was no way of proving he'd stolen the other stuff.

But that night Judy and I just laughed—a little nervously—and talked about how terrible it was that people try to steal things right out from under you. We shared a beer; it was the first alcohol Judy had had during her pregnancy, but we figured the baby could handle a few sips. My tongue didn't hurt at all, and I kept talking until Judy's yawns started to run together. She finally went back to bed, but I stayed up, walking around the house, picking up the nightstick, weighing it in my hands, putting it back down beside the door. I'd thought for sure the officers would take it, but they didn't. I'd thought for sure I'd feel bad about hitting the guy so hard, but I didn't.

I flicked on the light in the baby's room and sat there on the floor for a while, pleased. It looked pretty good, and I congratulated myself on that final coat of enamel. It was funny how the last coat had been exactly the right amount for the room. Since the latex was thinner, a third of a gallon had been left over, but the enamel gave out with the last brush stroke on the closet door.

I looked at the closet door, closed, and tried to remember the last time I'd seen it open. It had been closed for three days. It had been closed the whole time I was painting the baby's room. Christ, I thought: How could I have forgotten to paint the closet?

I started to go downstairs to find the latex, right then and there, driven by that same panic that had burned in me for days, but I only got as far as the door. Something stopped me. I heard Judy's light snore from our bedroom and knew I still had tomorrow.

# Kafka's Sister

Richard couldn't eat. The chapatis were too dry, and the curried soy beans and the eggplant were too hot. Some of his meals in India had been so spicy they'd made his gums bleed, and after four months he'd already lost fifteen pounds. He licked his fingers—he hadn't seen a fork since the Salvation Army hostel in Calcutta—and watched the setting sun streak the sky with fiery lines of color over the dusty plain behind the Japanese Zen shrine a quarter of a mile away.

He sat alone on the small verandah at the back of the government guest house. The lantern on the wall stunk of kerosene, and that didn't help his appetite any. Not that it mattered. He planned to start a fast the next day—the first day of his meditation at Goinka's ashram. So maybe he'd start a little early. Time wasn't a big concern now that he'd reached Bodh Gaya, the village where Buddha received his enlightenment. Every Buddhist nation had a temple here to accommodate pilgrims, but Richard doubted much else had changed in the past few thousand years.

There was, of course, the irony of Richard traveling halfway around the world from Euclid Street in D.C. only to discover that

Goinka was in the States at an ashram in Boulder, but the orange-robed monk at the temple had assured Richard that afternoon that they had all Goinka's lessons on tape. Not to worry. Come tomorrow in the hour before dawn. Bring a pillow.

Richard sipped his chai. He thumbed through a biography of Franz Kafka that his Australian friend Bryan had given him that morning. He thought about Bryan and supposed they were friends. A week together in India probably qualified them, and anyway Richard had given Bryan a book by Ram Dass in the exchange. Plus they had ridden together on the train from Calcutta, actually on top of the train, where they ate a lot of dust but at least were able to escape the crush of bodies, and the crying babies, and the smell of shit, and the rotting old men chewing their betel nuts and staining their chins red with the juice. They had argued that morning, though, when Richard dropped coins into every beggar's cup at the station. It was the politics of poverty.

When Richard looked up from his book, the sun was gone. The Japanese flooded the barren stretch around their shrine with strings of colored lanterns, and fingers of green and violet, yellow and blue reached into the darkness. Richard's kerosene lantern cast its own circle of light off the verandah. He sat and he waited.

He wasn't surprised when the visitors appeared. They materialized out of the darkness as naturally as the setting sun, and Richard was aware of their first movements, conscious of their shuffling gait, before the light introduced them. There were two, one carrying the other balanced on his hip like a bundle of rags. The smaller child was a stick figure, a caricature. Brittle limbs hung at raw angles from the blanket draped loosely around its body. The length of the child's arms and legs proved it wasn't an infant, but there was no way of telling a true age or even a sex. The child's round head lay against the other boy's shoulder, and lifeless eyes stared at the world. The blanket couldn't begin to hide the child's distended stomach, which stuck out grotesquely, almost comically, a balloon stretched past the bursting point. The other boy—thin, brown, peering expectantly through matted strands of hair—gripped the child with one long arm and held out an empty tin cup with the other.

As silently as the request was made, Richard took the cup and filled it with the leftovers of his meal. He handed it back over the rail. The older child seized the food, and the children disappeared.

As they left, Richard heard other footsteps, behind him.

"You can't feed them all, mate."

It was Bryan, leaning in the doorway off the verandah, legs crossed, arms folded.

"Came by to say no hard feelings for this morning," the Australian said. "I get carried away sometimes playing the cynic, but you've gotta watch this place. They eat bleeding hearts for lunch. You read some of that Kafka, you'll see what I mean. Beyond the grasp of the Western brain. People turning into cockroaches. Hunger Artists starving for the hell of it."

Richard said he wondered if Bryan hadn't missed some essential parts of the message—about Kafka, maybe about everything—but Bryan laughed. "Gotta go. Train to catch. Be back through in a month. See you if you're still around."

Richard wanted to call out, to ask Bryan to stay, but he couldn't find the words quickly enough, and then the Australian was gone. Bryan reminded Richard of his brother Del, who played rhythm guitar and electric rake in a band called Faithless. When they weren't touring clubs, Del gave music lessons to junior high school kids with black punk-dyed hair. Richard himself had been an employment counselor back in the States. They tended toward extremes in his family. His father was a Methodist minister who thought both sons were atheists; his mother coached girls' basketball and lived for the game.

The only thing not white about Richard as he stumbled through the dark up the road to the temple the next morning was the gray blanket around his shoulders. Cotton T-shirt, drawstring pajama pants, even his tennis shoes matched the thin thread of light that outlined the hills of Rajgir, ten miles away, hills backlit by a coming sun that already crowned Calcutta and warmed the Bay of Bengal several hundred miles east.

Richard turned off the road and slipped through a narrow gate and into the garden of Goinka's ashram, where he joined more white figures floating silently toward the temple. Though they were all Westerners, no one spoke, no one hurried. All followed the same pattern, raising one leg slowly, deliberately, then stepping carefully a short pace, making certain the foot was settled before drawing the other leg forward. All heads bent toward the ground. Most of the worshippers clasped hands behind their backs as they merged and separated, twisted and turned along the maze-like paths of the ashram garden.

Richard imitated their walk, following across the garden, up the steps of the temple, then around the temple to a stone patio on the north side, where they all faced east before a large steel gong. They assumed the lotus position, and one young man, a European like the rest, rose and struck the gong with a wooden mallet. The morning meditation began.

Richard closed his eyes, delaying the dawn, and he focused on his breathing as Goinka's book instructed, drawing air slowly, rhythmically through his nostrils. He felt his lungs swell against his ribs, expanding his chest. He imagined the fresh supply of oxygen coursing through his body and tried to picture the perfect chemical exchange in his cells, although that was a little difficult. He opened his mouth to allow the deflating bellows a channel for expelling each cycled breath.

Two roosters, one on either side of the village, screamed to announce a new day. "Crowing, crowing, crowing." Richard identified the sound, gave it a name, then let it go, letting his mind travel back to his breathing, reestablishing his focus, drinking deeply of the cool morning air, which carried a hint of moisture and tasted almost sweet after all the dusty heat he and Bryan had swallowed on the train. Richard tasted the smoke of cow-chip fires drifting down from the village, and he thought about camping with his father and his brother, about boats in rivers and fires on shores. He thought about his father's boats all lined up now and covered with tarps in the backyard of his father's house. A johnboat and a sailboat and a canoe—small boats a man could afford on a minister's salary. They had always camped near water so Richard's father could teach the boys how to handle the boats properly. "Only Jesus could walk on the water," he told them, mocking himself in his Sunday sermon voice. The smoke fired other memories, but Richard caught himself again. "Smoke, smoke, smoke." He straightened his back, shifted into a more comfortable position on his folded blanket, and wished he'd taken the monk's advice and brought a pillow instead.

Breathe in, breathe out; breathe in, breathe out—he repeated the instructions to himself and he tried counting breaths, but that was its own distraction, Richard soon realized, so he stopped counting and returned to the rise and fall of his diaphragm, what Goinka called his *chi*.

He thought about his father's boats again. There was a canoe they bought one winter when Richard was eight or nine. A yellow fiberglass canoe. Richard remembered the first trip with his father steering in the back while Richard and Del took turns paddling in front until their fingers were too numb from the wet and the cold. They camped in a grove of maples by a wide bend in the river where they hung fatigue-green army jungle hammocks between the trees. Richard wanted to sleep on the ground next to the fire, but his father wouldn't let him. In the night, late, he crawled out of his hammock, though, and pulled his sleeping bag next to the embers of the fire. He put more wood on and blew until it caught, then he fell asleep in his bag as the fire danced beside him. The last thing Richard remembered that night was the warmth of the fire on one cheek and the stinging cold of winter on the other.

And then he remembered being awake again. Someone was twisting his arm, hurting him, shouting at him. Richard was in the air, flying, falling, hitting the ground, and he saw his father running to the river with the fire trailing him. His father was pulling the fire, throwing it into the river. It hissed in the water, and Richard smelled singed hair, and he touched his face and knew it was his own. Del never woke up, just snored in his hammock between two maples. Richard's father came back from the river and spoke, angrily, his face twisted and purple, but it was as if Richard had suddenly gone deaf. He just nodded, and then watched while his father pulled his own sleeping bag out to share with Richard a safe distance from the fire.

"Father, father, father." Richard returned to his breathing, or tried to, but somewhere below his *chi* his stomach rumbled, and he remembered giving away most of his dinner the night before. "Hunger, hunger, hunger, hunger, hunger." He held the word, repeated it longer than he had the others, but this one was harder to let go. A dirty face peered up at him through a tangle of head lice and hair, and he saw another child's face, a face with unseeing eyes opened wide, opened for nothing. In Calcutta, Bryan had told him begging was a business, that parents break their children's bones, then set them wrong deliberately so they grow back twisted, crippled.

Richard tasted salt on his lips and only then felt the tears sliding over his cheeks. "Tears, tears, tears." He repeated the word, and then let it go. This time it was easier to follow his breathing, easier to fix his mind on the *chi,* easier to center himself, easier to block out the distractions. The rumbling of a cart, the sing-song chant of the village children now playing outside the ashram walls, the chatter of morning birds, the blare of a bus horn—Richard heard them, admitted them, allowed them to pass. Even the sound of the gong was noted and freed. The breeze of fellow pilgrims as they rose and swept past told him that the sitting had ended, but he stayed half an hour longer before walking in the garden with the others. The rest of the morning he spent sitting and meditatively walking, correcting himself when his mind wandered, chiding himself gently when he strayed.

At midday he returned to the guest house, accepting only a biscuit and some tea for lunch. He didn't eat the biscuit, and he slept through the heat of the day. Richard tried reading the book Bryan had given him, but he was distracted. The narrative eluded him so that Kafka's biography seemed to be a collection of stray facts rather than the story of a life. Franz Kafka hated his father, and once as an adult wrote a forty-five-page letter telling him why. Franz Kafka worked all his life at the Workmen's Accident Insurance Institute in Prague. Franz Kafka audited engineering courses for his job and learned about torture machines. Franz Kafka never married. Franz Kafka was born a Jew but declined to practice the religion.

Richard flipped some pages—to a passage on Kafka's youngest sister, whose name was Ottla and who was closest to him, though she was estranged from the rest of the family. Ottla married and had children. She survived Kafka into the war. She divorced her gentile husband when the Jews were being interned, realizing that as a single woman and thus officially a Jew she would be arrested, too. They put her in a camp near Prague at first—not a bad place. She might even have spent the war there. Most of the Kafkas lived through it, after all. But that didn't happen, because shortly after her arrest, Ottla volunteered, full-knowing, to escort a children's transport to the death camp at Auschwitz.

Richard closed Bryan's book.

Again that evening he sat alone on the verandah. He drank his chai but touched none of the food. He sat patiently in his straight-back chair to watch the sunset, and he imagined an unbroken string of spectacular desert sunsets, melancholy dusks as the Japanese filled the night with their carnival rows of color. Richard, with his lantern, was secure in his own outpost of light. He waited.

Soon they came, and again he heard them before he saw them: a clean step followed by a hesitating one; a foot scuffing the dirt, a toe stubbed on a rock, a sure step, then a dragging one. The children assumed form as they entered the circle of light, and as before, the younger one, wrapped loosely in rags, was propped motionless on the hip of the older boy. The cup was raised, accepted, filled, returned, but no words were exchanged, and the children's stony expressions never wavered, even when Richard spoke the Hindi greeting, "*Namaste.*" The older boy turned slowly away from the verandah and stepped into the night, but as they vanished Richard thought he saw the smaller child's head tilt slightly toward the food.

After they left, Richard tried to write a letter to the people he'd worked with in D.C., but he couldn't get past the salutation. His girlfriend, Claire—his ex-girlfriend—had quit the social service collective the year before to go to law school, and now he couldn't think of who to address the letter to. He tried Bryan's line, "Dear Bleeding Hearts," but that didn't work either.

At Euclid Street, with donations and grants, they had started a neighborhood association and brought in legal aid to work for tenants' rights. They had done welfare referral. Richard counseled teenagers about jobs. The big three-story house could accommodate a lot. On Thursdays they held a pediatrics clinic. They even put a recreation room in the basement. That was why nothing seemed odd when two men came up to the office one day six months ago looking for ping-pong balls. After they got Richard into the supply closet, though, they shut the door behind him, slamming his face into the wall. The typewriter, the petty cash box, and a television from upstairs were gone by the time he got out. It was the third robbery in a year, and he applied for his passport the next day.

Richard put down his pen and paper. Maybe he'd write tomorrow.

When he thought about it, Richard relished the sameness of the days that followed. The ritualistic walk in the predawn hour, the hint of sunrise before he closed his eyes at the sound of the temple gong, the single cup of chai he allowed himself at midday and then again in the evening, his solitary view of the sunset—those subtle activities added to his routine of fasting and meditation and provided a kind of structure for the day.

On the third morning Richard stumbled into one of the dried bushes in the ashram garden when a wave of dizziness struck suddenly. Thorns pricked a dozen tiny scratches on his arm. He drank more water after that, and he began resting more often in the afternoons. Reading brought headaches, he soon discovered, and writing seemed pointless, so he gave that up too. He lost weight quickly; he grew pale.

And every evening the beggars came. On the fifth night, the older boy laid the small child on the ground and scraped Richard's meal into the cup himself; he stuffed in all he could and ate the rest there by the verandah. When he placed a bite in his companion's mouth, the child hesitated at first, then slowly worked his jaws around the food.

The process for Richard was a sort of easing out of himself, of leaving the old Richard in a distant place that had outlived its usefulness, its feasibility. Before Bodh Gaya, for a long time, Richard had thought of himself as a war veteran—something like those men who had been to Vietnam and hated it, and yet still wore their army jackets to get them through winters ten years later. A high lottery number had kept him out of the Vietnam draft, but he had fought anyway—he had fought the government. Most of the others at the Euclid Street house had fought, too, and the battle had escalated over the years as they felt themselves assaulted on more and more fronts, drawn into other conflicts. Richard had believed for a time in the strength of their will and the rightness of their causes; he had even thought, briefly, that they had the upper hand. But there were other forces he hadn't reckoned with, and he had started thinking that maybe history was being shaped somewhere else, somewhere beyond them.

On some days early in the fast, he felt a kind of desperation, a frustrated need to be heard, and an image of Kafka's sister haunted him like a thing just outside his vision he couldn't turn quite fast enough to see. He felt like a man pinned against a wall by an invisible opponent, and he remembered a picture of a test pilot strapped into place in a wind tunnel, his face to the wind. Thick goggles protected his eyes, but the blast still flattened his features, pulled violently at his flesh, parted his lips, forced his mouth open, pressed the loose skin back toward his cheeks, bared the pilot's teeth and gums. He looked like a man who wanted to shout, louder than any jet, but any shout he might have mustered was flattened, compressed against the back of his throat, trapped.

But that passed too.

Some evenings Richard stayed late at the ashram after meditation to listen to the tapes of Goinka's lessons, but he grew less and less inclined to make conversation with the Europeans there, and as he grew weaker with the fast he decided he needed the time to rest. He suffered periods of nausea when stomach cramps and vertigo struck together, and on the tenth day he interrupted the morning sitting when he suddenly clutched his stomach and bent forward gagging. On the thirteenth day a German boy followed him from the ashram and caught Richard on the road to the guest house.

"May I walk with you?"

Richard nodded.

"I leave tomorrow—I go to New Delhi—and I thought if you like we might travel together, and if you are ill you could get medicine there."

"But I'm not ill," Richard said.

"But I thought—this is hard for me," the German continued. "But you are alone and never speak to us. You take everything so seriously, and we—most of us—we are here just to see what it is, I think. And I must tell you that you don't look well. You are so thin and your face has little color. The others have made a joke about the American, but I worry for you."

Richard smiled at the German and said, "Maybe the path to truth is paved with suffering."

"Maybe," the German said, stopping in the road. "But how much suffering? The Buddha teaches a Middle Way."

Richard walked on alone.

That night the smaller child reached for the cup once it was filled and placed a handful of food into its own mouth. Richard put a separate cup of milk on the rail, and the young beggars drank greedily. The older boy seemed to smile as they left.

A week later the two walked separately to the verandah; the smaller child held his brother's hand and moved unsteadily, but still walked under his own power. Both were boys, Richard decided. He brought them extra food in addition to the milk.

His own hunger cut like a rusty knife in the third week of the fast, but though the jagged pain made sleep difficult, it no longer seemed to matter. Richard spent his nights lying in his bed, but awake, waiting for the morning. At times now he saw the world with astonishing clarity. He studied the swirling wood patterns on the floor of the guest house. He saw the dried, intertwining branches in the temple garden as secret maps. He saw intricate relationships, vital connections where none had existed before, and it frightened him and it thrilled him. But just as often his vision blurred; sharp edges appeared dull and ill defined; he bumped into things and had trouble seeing at a distance.

On the twenty-first day village children taunted the *angrezi* during the evening meditation and threw rocks over the ashram wall. A sharp stone struck Richard's face, but he ignored the blow until he felt himself being lowered onto his back while European hands worked to stop the flow of blood that drained from the gash in his cheek. A circle of worried faces greeted Richard when he opened his eyes, but he insisted on walking back to the guest house alone. He waited until the beggars came for their dinner before he crawled into bed.

The next morning he fell on his way to the temple, reopening the bandaged wound. It occurred to Richard that perhaps he should break his fast soon, and he remembered the reflection that had startled him earlier as he left the guest house. A face stripped of light, a skull draped with sagging flesh had met his sunken eyes when he passed a darkened window that mirrored the man he'd become. He lifted himself from the road and stumbled on to the ashram. During the morning sitting he slumped forward and drifted for a time out of consciousness. After the sitting he returned to the guest house, falling twice more on the way, and for the next three days he stayed in bed, rising only in the evenings to take his meals to the verandah for the boys.

Though still too thin, the brothers had filled out quickly with a regular diet. Distended stomachs, hollow eyes—the signs of malnutrition faded. Flesh appeared on bony arms and legs. Some strength returned to atrophied muscles. Frozen faces regained expression. On the twenty-fifth day, when Richard dropped the tray and slumped to the verandah floor, the children climbed under the rail and, with his nodding guidance, led him back to his room. They helped him into bed, then they scooped up his watch and a pile of rupees lying on his bedside stand. Their feet slapped lightly on the floorboards as they hurried from the guest house and into the dark.

"Hungry, mate?"

At first the words echoed like nonsense syllables. Hungry? The dull ache in Richard's stomach, the hollow, muted craving seemed to have passed on to a dimension that defied fulfillment. He had always been hungry; he would always be hungry. Hunger colored all thought; it shaped all vision. He shook his head; he wanted to shake his head—he couldn't be certain if the order had followed proper channels and been carried out. The question was repeated several times, calmly but insistently, before it occurred to Richard that he might open his eyes and identify the speaker.

"Hungry, mate?" This time Bryan didn't wait for Richard to respond. Once he saw Richard was awake, the Australian lifted Richard's head and tucked the edge of a mug between his lips.

"You'd better like it. It's dinner." Richard sipped the broth, slowly at first, swallowing gingerly. Bryan restrained him when he tried to gulp too fast. "You'll be sick if you're not careful now. A little at a time. A little at a time. How long since you ate, anyway? You look like one of those bloody saddhus that poke their eyeballs out so they can sit by the road with a beggar's cup."

As soon as he finished with the soup, Richard leaned over the side of the bed and threw up. A few minutes later Bryan was back with another mug. "What say we try it again, eh?" Richard held the soup down the second time, and he even managed to eat a few biscuits before falling asleep. Bryan roused him a couple of times during the night and forced him to drink large glasses of fruit juice, and when Richard awoke the next morning Bryan was back with his biscuits and soup and juice, pouring them down Richard's throat until Richard pushed his hand away and insisted on feeding himself.

"Well, mate, looks like a fine bloody mess you've got yourself into." Bryan sprawled in a chair beside the bed.

Richard attempted a smile.

"Nothing to worry about now," Bryan said. "We're getting you out of here. Meditation ain't good for your health. You'll be turning into that cockroach next thing you know."

"I don't want to leave," Richard croaked, his voice stiff from disuse. "I can't leave."

"Bloody hell to that."

"Someone's got to take care of the boys." Panic laced Richard's voice. "And I'm learning so much." His voice trembled and broke.

Bryan rose, scowling, and he began stuffing Richard's clothes into a rucksack. He gathered Richard's papers and passport, picked up the Kafka book with two hands—it could have been a Bible— then rolled up Richard's sleeping bag. He kicked Goinka's book across the floor.

"No martyrs, Richard. There ain't no bleeding martyrs."

The afternoon bus carried them ten miles to Rajgir. They could catch the train from there, Bryan said, when Richard was ready to travel farther. Though they spoke little after that, Richard accepted the food set before him, and he slept through the afternoon and most of the night. Once he woke up thinking he had to carry his tray to the young beggars, but there was no tray, no verandah, no beggars. He dreamed of the temple, and he saw Indian children instead of the white-robed Europeans walking the ashram garden. When he tried to open the gate he discovered they'd locked him out; no one came when he knocked, and his cries went unanswered.

The next night he dreamed he was playing basketball at the junior high on Euclid Street. He was trying to get his team to pass the ball around, set up some plays the way his mother had taught him the game—short passes, double screens, pick and roll. But all they wanted to do was block shots and shoot. Frustrated, he drove the lane himself. Three men moved to swat down anything he might send up, and he managed to smile as he shoveled the ball off to a teammate left free on the other side of the hoop.

Bryan shook him awake before dawn. "Can you walk?" Richard nodded; his own voice sounded too strange to him just yet, and he let Bryan help him out of bed.

"Follow me then," Bryan said. "There's something I think you'd like to see."

Richard's legs held steady, and he only leaned on Bryan's arm a little as they padded slowly out of the mud-brick hotel and up the dry road behind Rajgir. Every morning for a month Richard had seen the dawn from Bodh Gaya as a trace of light behind the Rajgir hills, and he wondered now what sunrise would look like from Rajgir itself.

A stone wall marked the side of what seemed to be a temple set into the side of one of the hills. Bryan said it was a Hindu shrine, and he led Richard to a stairway up the side. Several times as they climbed they had to stop and lean against the wall until Richard caught his breath, but Bryan was patient, holding his arm at the elbow and guiding him slowly up the steps.

Smokey torches lit the stone terrace at the top, and all along a short wall pressed into the hill Hindu women washed themselves and their children in the warm water that steamed out of a series of spouts. Richard thought he could see the shapes of the houses and shops of Rajgir below them, but he saw no light from Bodh Gaya off in the western darkness. Bryan paused at a wide opening in the terrace, where more steps led underground. A fine mist rose from the opening like a soft breath on their faces as they stood at the top looking in. Two brown men passed them and descended into the hole.

"Go ahead, mate," Bryan said. "I've already been."

Richard hesitated.

"Well, go on then."

Dim lanterns guided Richard down the stone steps, and he trailed a cautious hand on a rock wall of the pit, which was sunk deep into the ground where the hot sulfur water seeped through the earth's brittle crust. The steps turned, then continued under the steaming water at the bottom, where Richard joined a noisy group of brown men who were bathing and worshipping a small orange-painted statue on a shelf cut into a corner of the wall. They chanted prayers to their god. Richard watched and listened. The water came up to his chest, but he floated on his back close to the side, and he looked straight up past forty feet of stone to a square patch of blue-black sky. He lay there for a long time, waiting, and the stars faded like old prayers, lost, as the pitch gave way to the soft glow of morning.

# Adam's House

"Women," my brother Adam says as he taps in a quarter-inch shim between the post and the beam, and I know exactly what he means. Adam lays his hammer on the top of the ladder, then he steadies the twelve-foot four-by-four we're using for a brace. I lower the jack. The beam groans, then settles onto the newly shimmed post, and I grab the four-by-four before Adam lets it go.

We've been shimming the posts to even up the deck around Adam's house. It's been six years since he last did any work on the place, and now he wants to finish it, and the first thing Adam wants to do is frame in a porch where the deck is. Some of the posts have settled slightly over the past six years—Adam's got the house on stilts because his land borders Black Creek Swamp—so we've got to shim first or the porch roof won't come out even.

We must have spent an hour already today siting points with a surveyor's transit to make sure the measurements are right—Adam working the transit while I moved the marker. It was almost like being back in military school—Adam giving orders in the same clear, certain way he used to march all us cadets around on the drill field. Stomachs in, chests out, chin-straps tight, epaulets straight, shiny boots reflecting the afternoon sun. And Adam in command.

Adam has been telling me about him and Donna; they've sort of split up, which is why he's back working on his house. Or maybe they've sort of split up because he's back here working on his house. It's hard to say for sure, but I think they've sort of split up because Donna got him to keep her daughter, Annie, for a long weekend—by himself—while Donna went off to a bee-keepers' convention. Suddenly, after two years, that made it more of a relationship than Adam wanted—too close to parenthood, too close to settling down—even though he's practically lived at Donna's house for the past year and a half. Adam's got a room he uses sometimes in the house here—visquine windows and a leaky wood stove—and he set up a kitchen in what was sup-posed to be a workshop on the ground under the house. But life's a little easier at Donna's place in town. Out here he doesn't even have indoor plumbing; fortunately he doesn't have any neighbors either.

Adam started out building a hell of a house, and he'll be the first to admit that he overbuilt the place. For instance, the bolts he's got holding the floor beams to the posts are so strong they can handle double the pressure of the boards around them. Every stick of wood here is pressure treated, and if you count ground level and the sleeping loft, Adam's house is four stories, which may well make it the tallest one-bedroom house in America.

"It was the pressure to be there all the time," Adam says.

I don't say anything, because as I lower the jack Adam forgets to hold the four-by-four and that twelve footer topples like a tree, almost hitting me in the shoulder. It crashes onto the hard dirt under the house and raises a puff of black dust.

Adam scrambles down the ladder. "Sorry, Wayne," he says. I say that's OK.

It's funny how when Adam screws up he says he's sorry and it's forgotten, but whenever I screw up I get a lecture and then I have to prove myself all over again. That's why Adam's on the ladder and I'm on the ground: at first I was knocking in the shims, but I left my hammer on the top step and it fell when I moved the ladder.

"You know what the number one cause of accidents is with ladders?" he asked then, handing me the jack.

"Falling off," I answered, wishing he wouldn't say.

"It's forgetting things on top and having them fall on you." Adam's lectures are usually very short, but he has them for every occasion. He'll never say anything to me in front of other people, though. Even in military school he'd save his lectures until we were alone. Once during inspection he told me to recite the serial number on my gun—we called our guns "dicklesses," because the firing mechanisms had been removed. I made up a number and he knew it, but instead of calling me out in front of the company he dragged me out of bed late that night and made me run stadium steps for an hour.

Adam moves the ladder over, lifting it as effortlessly as if it were a pencil. He still has those broad swimmer's shoulders—he swam butterfly in college—and even though I'm slightly taller than he is, I still feel like I have to look up to see his face. Adam holds the four-by-four in place while I work the jack again. Another post, another shim.

I have a son, Lucas, but he doesn't live with me. If he were here, though, I could put him in charge of the hammer so we'd always know where it is.

Actually Adam didn't need to tell me about him and Donna. I already knew because Donna told me. She called me the day after Adam announced he was going to be staying in his visquine room full time, and she cried a little over the phone.

"He's your brother—you tell me. Is he seeing somebody else? Does he want another girlfriend?"

It was a familiar conversation, one I've had several times over the past several years with different women Adam had been seeing. I didn't think I'd be having it with Donna, though. I didn't think I'd be telling her the problem was with my brother, not her—that he just has these demons in him that won't let him be.

I don't know why they always make me their confidante, as if I have nothing better to do with my life than pick up the broken pieces. But I always tell them what they want to hear. I told Donna what she wanted to hear, not that it made her feel any better. I could sense it happening even then, though: as long as she has me to talk to she thinks there'll be some hope for her and Adam. And how do I know she's not right? Winter's coming; cold weather has a way of rekindling romance, and I seriously doubt we'll have this house wired and insulated before spring. On the other hand, Adam has a very warm down sleeping bag that's been tested at ten below, and north Florida never gets nearly that cold—even out here in the woods.

I told Donna I'd drop by if she wanted me to, and she said she'd like that, she'd like to talk some more, maybe she'd fix us some dinner. She said Annie would like to see me, too. Her daughter, Annie, is four—not quite as old as my son, Lucas.

It's taking us a long time to shim these posts. There are sixteen of them—fat, round telephone poles supporting the deck on two sides of the house—and we've still got to go back and drill new bolt holes. I'll do that myself while Adam builds the frames for the walls. I think we're going to need a third person to help us raise the frames once he's got them together. He says we can do it ourselves, though, so I guess that means we'll try.

This was going to be his and his wife Jennifer's house originally. They got quite a lot done in the two years before she left him. There again I think the house might have been partly at fault. Adam designed it and got more and more wrapped up in the construction as they went along. He hooked up floodlights and extension cords from the utility pole out by the dirt road, and he'd be stringing plumb lines and nailing up bird blocking hours after Jennifer had brushed the sawdust out of her hair and retired to the back seat of their car. After awhile she found some other things she'd rather do than work on the house, so Adam called me up to help him, just like I knew he eventually would.

Actually I'd been biding my time, wondering if he was going to need me at all. God knows I needed him then—the woman I was living with had just told me she was pregnant—but the way we've always been I've got to wait for Adam to make the first move. It just doesn't work if I try to force it. I suppose that's one thing wrong with the women Adam sees: they reach a plateau eventually where Adam's natural restraint comes out and the relationship stalls. Maybe if they didn't try to push things any further, Adam would be fine and the relationship might go on forever at a pleasant enough level—pleasant for Adam, anyway. But they want more. They finally say, "Adam, why don't we—"

And a couple of days later they're on the phone to me.

So I took Jennifer's place. That was six and a half years ago. Bobbie—the woman I was living with—was already three months pregnant when she told me about it, and she said there was no way she would have a second trimester abortion. She didn't think we should get married, either, even though I offered. Instead she had this crazy idea that she should have the baby and if it was a girl she'd keep it and if it was a boy the child would be mine. I didn't understand she might actually mean that, so I spent the pregnancy trying to be a good husband when maybe I should have been pre-paring for something else.

Bobbie didn't think much of Adam, which always surprised me. I just naturally assume that everyone who meets Adam is going to be impressed with him—most people are—and I'm always surprised with people who aren't. I tend to want to get to know peo-ple like that almost in a scientific sort of way.

For six months I drove out to Adam's house every day after work. He was always there when I arrived. Bobbie and the house grew at about the same rate, while Jennifer just seemed to drop out of sight like one of those missing persons. I heard a rumor that she was seeing a mental health counselor.

When Jennifer told Adam she wanted a divorce, she simply showed up at the house one day. I remember we were nailing in the steps from the second floor to the third, which is really just half a floor. Adam was working the Skil saw out on the deck and I was nailing the boards he cut, so I watched their conversation through a window above. They both must have known what was coming by then—they'd been drifting for several months—but I was still kind of surprised by the lack of expression on Adam's face. They could have been having a business conversation. Maybe they were. Adam mostly listened—I couldn't hear what they were saying—and after Jennifer left he pulled down his safety visor, put on the ear protectors, and turned on the Skil saw. It was ten minutes before I realized he wasn't cutting anything, and all I was hearing was the high whine of the saw while the blade sliced nothing but air just inches away from Adam's white hands.

A week later Adam and I put visquine over all the holes in the house—the window frames, the doorways, a couple of unfinished walls. He didn't say anything, he just moved along efficiently with the staple gun, hanging the plastic sheets, but somehow I knew we weren't going to be working on the house anymore.

Bobbie had a Caesarean section two weeks after that. It was a boy, and we named him Lucas. Lucas was born deaf. Bobbie had had high blood pressure, but the doctors assured us that high blood pressure didn't cause the deafness, although they couldn't be sure what did. Bobbie hadn't had German measles or anything; her diet had been good. She was as sad about Lucas as I was, but she still wouldn't breastfeed him.

"I'm sorry, Wayne," she said before she even left the hospital. "But you might as well start him on the bottle."

Adam is still overbuilding. He could have used a two-by-ten for the hip rafter—the rafter that runs diagonally from the corner of the house to the corner of the new porch wall—but he insisted on a four-by-ten. More stability, he says. Yeah, I agree, and hell to raise. I've never lifted anything so heavy in my life as a nineteen-foot four-by-ten. Now we're putting up the rest of the rafters, and I'm bending too many nails trying to toenail my ends onto the beam along the top of the porch wall. Working there puts me right at the edge of the deck, and the truth is I'm nervous because I've got to hang out over the beam about half the time, and there's a twenty-foot drop from there to the ground. Adam thinks it's my technique.

"Just blunt the end of the nail with your hammer first. It won't bend so easy." Adam is up on scaffolding working the band board end of the rafters. He has to toenail, too, but he never seems to have much trouble.

It seems a little strange that we're building more onto the house—adding this porch—instead of just finishing what's already been started, what's been neglected for six years. But that's just Adam's way. He wants the porch done—roofed, shingled, and screened—before we move inside. Then, he says, everything that's in the house can go out on the porch and we'll be able to work inside without all the obstructions. Uh huh, I say. And why can't we just pile all Adam's stuff in the middle of the second floor, which is just one big room, and work around it?

Everything about this house is peculiar. Probably the strangest part is the outside stairs, which lead up from the ground, a fourteen-foot rise. Instead of coming straight up, perpendicular to the deck or running parallel to the house to a landing on the deck level, the stairs start several feet from the house, rise five feet to a landing moving diagonally away from the house, then come back up to the deck. It looks like a giant check mark. All because Adam didn't want to cut down a tree.

This I think is crazy when you consider that Adam's house sits in the middle of a forest. It's hard to understand how any one tree more or less can make much difference, but Adam says his hop hornbeam has integrity. He says it's an understory tree, which means it's not the dominant tree in the forest. It grows under the larger trees—the oaks, primarily—but it has its own niche; or, as Adam says, it holds its maturity. So it grows in the crook of the bent arm of the stairs, almost as if Adam designed the whole house around it. The hop hornbeam's thin trunk doesn't sprout branches until about ten feet, and there doesn't seem to be much special about its dull bark or its smooth, waxy leaves. I keep staring at it, thinking one day I'll see something in that hop hornbeam that I'm missing, but so far it's still just a tree to me. It doesn't even flower like a dogwood or a redbud.

Adam's getting impatient with me because I'm working so slowly, but there's nothing I can do about it. I've never been comfortable with heights, and I think I'm doing pretty well just being up here. If Adam had his way he'd probably do the whole thing by himself. He'd spend hours planing down rough-cut lumber. He'd measure everything to within a sixteenth of an inch or not build at all. He'd use materials of such high quality that the house would never get finished, it'd cost him so much to buy everything.

I'm surprised he settled for number three boards for roofing the porch. A grade that low—especially for tongue-and-groove board—means you're going to end up using some bad wood, and you're even going to throw some away. Of course, the more fundamental question is why not just use plywood for roofing your porch? You're still going to tarpaper it; you're still going to put down fascia; and you're still going to shingle. Plywood will keep you every bit as dry, though maybe not as warm and maybe not as long. It's going to take us through tomorrow to cover these rafters with all that tongue-and-groove board. If we were using plywood we'd probably be able to finish today. And plywood is one hell of a lot cheaper, even than number three grade. I suppose since Adam's roofing with boards he'll have a much stronger roof when he's through—one he can insulate if he wants to close in his porch and add extra rooms, not that I think he'll ever want to.

I mentioned that to Donna last night when I stopped by, and I could tell by her hopeful expression that probably I shouldn't have. We were eating bean loaf and a sprout salad. Donna was telling me what a mystery Adam is, as if I didn't know. Little Annie was asking for a slice of the fresh banana bread that sat on the stove. I was wondering if Adam, alone in the woods, was working on the house yesterday evening without me.

I had been there before—with one of Adam's old girlfriends. Not once, actually, but a couple of times, and it always started out similar to what was happening with Donna: with dinner to talk about Adam. Then maybe we'd have some beers together a week or so later. Then there'd be questions about Adam when he and I were growing up. Questions about his marriage to Jennifer. Questions about the house. And then, gradually, there would be questions about me. Each time was a rerun—even the first time. I knew exactly what I would do before I did it, and I knew how they would respond. I knew when they would call and where I would sit and how good and how bad the first kiss would feel. I was reading a script, and I knew it was a script, but I still couldn't put it down. I'd read it before; I had to know what came next. I saw one woman—Denise—for a couple of months before I had to break things off. She was the only one I actually slept with. I could never be sure if they were looking at me and seeing Adam, though. They probably were; it would only be natural. I could never be sure who I was looking at, either. They all thought I was being noble when I finally said that I couldn't go on, that I couldn't because of Adam, that it just wasn't right. They all thought I was being noble, and they all wanted to be friends—which apparently means an exchange of warm smiles in the grocery store but not much else. It was proof of my sensitivity, they all realized, that I wouldn't do anything that might hurt my brother, no matter what he might have done to them.

In a way, though, maybe I did want Adam to find out, although I never told him. I'm not exactly sure why—not sure why I might have wanted him to know, not sure why I never said anything. If he ever found out he never let me know about it. He probably doesn't suspect anything with me and Donna, and so far there's nothing to suspect. Last night I was just a friend—just her boyfriend's brother stopping by to talk.

It's funny how I couldn't be around Annie last night without thinking about Lucas. Lucas is six now, and he lives in St. Augustine. He still doesn't have any parents, but at least they've got him in that School for the Deaf and Blind. I've been over to see him a couple of times, and the last time I was there he showed me a horse he had carved. At least I assumed it was a horse: it had four legs and a long head, and Lucas seemed pretty proud of it. I galloped it all over him and me both when we sat out in the soft grass in front of the library. Lucas still can't talk; I'm not sure if he knows I'm his father or not. I always make sure I have toys whenever I go to see him so we can play together, so we don't have to stand around and feel awkward with nothing to do.

Once a couple of years ago I called Bobbie to see if she ever visited him—he was at a children's home in town then. She said no. She wasn't mean about it or anything; she just sounded like someone who'd made a decision and was trying to live with it and not feel too badly about things. Bobbie works for a newspaper recycler now. I see her company's trucks around town, but I never see her. She went to live with her sister right after Lucas was born. I kept him for all of two weeks before I had to give him up. It wasn't so much the difficulty of caring for him when he was an infant, although that was pretty hard, as it was the sadness I felt whenever I looked at him, knowing Lucas couldn't even hear himself cry.

Now when I see him I wonder what he knows, what he thinks about. He doesn't smile a lot. He's got a hearing aid, which is supposed to help some—no one can say exactly how much—and his teachers in St. Augustine say he appears to be very bright, even though they haven't made much progress in teaching him to communicate. Apparently he'll whittle all day as long as he's got his knife and a block of wood.

The rafters are all up, and we're putting in the bird blocking now. I'm working the Skil saw on the ground and Adam's nailing the blocks in, but I can hardly cut them fast enough to keep up with him. He wants to get them in place quickly so we can start on the roof today. Adam only has two speeds: deliberate and fast. Fast is what he uses once a decision's been made.

I'm sure Adam deliberated in his own way before he decided to break up with Donna and leave Annie to look for another father figure. It wouldn't have been a quick decision. More like the way he double measures everything, checking his tape on all the boards twice before he puts them to the saw. Measure twice, cut once is what he always says. After two years I thought he might actually stay with Donna, though—out of dumb animal habit if for no other reason. But he didn't, and he's a stubborn man. I doubt that the coldest winter in north Florida history will change his mind now.

She would still take him back in a heartbeat—I know she would. She thinks he's so strong . . . they all think he's so strong. Sometimes I think he might be weaker than any of us, though, and maybe what we worship as strength is really something very brittle, like a thing frozen so hard it runs the risk of shattering on contact. Sometimes I think he knows that, too.

It's strange to look up and see Adam on the rafters where I was working just a couple of hours ago. He almost seems reckless, the way he hangs over the edge to nail in that bird blocking. I want to turn off the saw and yell up to him, tell him to be careful. The drop from there to the ground is as far for him as it was for me, but he doesn't seem the least bit nervous about it. I wonder how much darker the house will be once we roof the porch. With the wide deck up high on the south and east sides, Adam's house has always caught plenty of sun, but the trees seem to crowd around it now. I wonder what Adam's going to do when the house is finished.

He was having trouble a few minutes ago toenailing in one of the blocks, and I noticed Adam pulled his bent nails out and started new holes with a drill. The nails went in cleanly after that. I sure could have used the drill when I was having problems with my end of the rafters. I guess there are still some things Adam has yet to tell me. This is my first time building a house, after all, and it's easy for him to forget what I don't know.

I was thinking about swinging by Donna's again on the way home from Adam's this evening. I was thinking maybe I would stay around just long enough for a cup of coffee. I know she'd like to see me, especially now, so soon after the breakup. Nobody likes to be alone.

But Adam can be infectious when he shifts his work gear into high, and I'm thinking now that maybe we can get this porch roof up tonight if I stick around. We can flip on the floodlights and hump it, as Adam likes to say. Once we get started on that tongue-and-groove, once we get our measurements down, it should go fairly quickly. Working together, we ought to be able to have this thing past the tarpaper stage by midnight. Tomorrow after work we can put down the fascia and shingle—if we're not too tired to stand.

I've got plenty of time later for visiting Donna. Time later for coffee. Plenty of time to get together for beers. Time for her questions. Time for her friendly hugs to turn into something warmer in the winter months ahead. I know what will happen. I can almost see the future with Donna as clearly as I can see this Skil saw blade bite into the wood I'm feeding it, as clearly as I can see it spit out the yellow sawdust in a heavy spray covering the maple leaves behind it on the ground.

But I have this other idea, too—this dream about me and Adam and Lucas. I'm thinking, what if we finished this porch roof, then went on ahead and closed it in? We could insulate, throw up some walls, make a couple of extra rooms for Lucas and me. Or just close in the porch on one side of the house. Lucas and I could share a room, and we wouldn't really be in Adam's way. Just us—just the guys. Adam and I could work at our leisure then to finish the house. And we would really finish it this time: wire and insulate, install plumbing fixtures, hang the sheetrock, and move the kitchen upstairs. We would rip out that visquine and hang some first-class doors and windows, replace that leaky wood stove with some central air and heat. There's no end to what we could do.

And Lucas. Lucas could whittle the whole damn forest down. He could turn down his hearing aid as low as he wanted. He could run around and be a little nature boy. He could follow after me and make sure I don't leave the hammer anywhere I shouldn't. He probably doesn't know what a family's supposed to be, anyway—he wouldn't think it strange and there'd be no one to tell him otherwise.

# Ice Age

In the winter, Roy the lifeguard nails blankets to walls. His baby, Sarah, lies wrapped in a quilt on top of the clothes dryer in the kitchen. Roy is in the living room, cold even with the heater, but he can still see her because the house is that small. The dryer is going, and the oven is on, lulling Sarah to sleep and keeping her asleep until Roy's hammering wakes her. He stops, leans his cheek against the living room wall. The house isn't insulated, and the wood is almost as cold as the icy air outside.

The morning's low was five degrees at the airport. Roy's wife, Anne, before she left for work, assured him it's always warmer in town, but he doesn't know if he believes her. He wonders why they always say it's colder at the airport. Anne teaches high school German; she enjoys teaching, even though the pay's no good. She quotes Goethe to Roy when she thinks he needs to learn a lesson. Earlier in the week, when Roy nailed plastic over the windows, she frowned, and asked if he knew Goethe's last words.

He shook his head—he couldn't speak because his mouth was full of nails—and she told him: "More light."

Roy spit out the nails and said he would ask for more heat if it came down to that for him. Roy is a lifeguard in the summer, but during the winter he tries to stay inside.

"When I was little," he told Anne, "they used to say, 'Would you rather burn to death or freeze?'"

"And you said burn?" Anne asked.

"Every time," said Roy.

Sarah sniffs; she sucks her red fingers. Roy taps his knee with the hammer, just to watch the reflex, until Sarah's eyes wilt closed.

There have been three deaths this week since the temperatures dropped so suddenly—all old people, all near Roy and Anne. The Sunday newspaper reported the first one:

John Brown, 74, of 863 Delaware St., was found dead Saturday night by a friend.

The victim was found lying face up on the floor in his bedroom next to a gas heater. He was wearing pants and two shirts, but no shoes. A jacket was next to his body.

When Brown expired, police said, he was apparently trying to start the heater. Police found several bits of paper in the heater.

So Roy closed off Sarah's room Sunday. He stuffed towels around the door to seal it. Sarah's been sleeping in the bed with Roy and Anne since then, but she makes noises in the night—little cries like she's dreaming. She's only three months old, though, and Roy wonders what there is to dream about when you're only three months old. Because she cries, Roy ends up on the too-short couch, where the cold drafts converge in the living room. There are cracks in the walls, spaces around the door, chips in the plaster that holds the windows.

On Monday, Roy pulled himself into the crawl space between the ceiling and the tin roof, where he stacked piles of newspapers for insulation. He'd taken the papers from a recycling bin after the newspaper that day announced a second death. They blamed hypothermia. The newspaper said police found a can of frozen soup inside the victim's house. Monday night, Roy heard the papers in the attic crackling with the wind that slipped under the eaves. He thought about how they used to just say: "He froze to death." Now they blame hypothermia, which means you worked up a sweat in the cold, the sweat evaporated, and as it evaporated it stole the heat from your body. Then you froze to death.

Tuesday was when Roy nailed visquine over the windows. Anne protested at first. She said they had to be able to see outside. That was when she quoted Goethe: *more light*. Roy said maybe she should have married Goethe. It was their first fight since Sarah was born, although it wasn't a very bad one. The cold always does this sort of thing to Roy, and they both know it.

Sarah was born in October—born the same day Roy turned thirty. It was also John Lennon's birthday, or would have been. He would have been forty-three. And John Lennon's son—Yoko and John's boy, Sean—he has the same birthday, too.

Roy's family has always gone in for auspicious birthdays. His sister's little boy was born on his mother's fiftieth birthday. Everybody says those two, Roy's mother and Roy's sister's boy, have a spiritual bond, something special between them that language can't touch. They live in Texas, in Dallas, where it's even colder than it is where Roy and Anne live. The newspaper says ice storms are shredding the phone lines out in Texas. Roy's brother-in-law lost his flat-roof garage last week when it collapsed under all the ice.

Roy and Anne are in south Georgia. There's little chance of ice storms there, but the cold still scares Roy. It's never been this cold before in the South—not in this century. The newspaper says in 1886 it was minus two degrees. It's eight out there now, without figuring in the wind-chill factor. Roy told Anne they should move down to Florida. She said that's silly, because they're practically in Florida now. Roy said he meant they should move to Key West, and she said that was impossible. He argued with her. Once when he had lived there they had a cold spell in January. Key West temperatures hit the low sixties and no one had heat in their homes. Roy thought that was funny, and just to prove how funny that was, he'd pulled on a sweater and slept on the beach at night. He met a man with iguanas. They were in the man's car, and the man had his heater running for them. The man said the sudden cold could kill the iguanas; he said they weren't used to it.

Roy met another man once, one who wasn't afraid of the cold. Roy and the man were both in a hospital in New York, in Queens, sitting in their wheelchairs in the day room watching a Knicks game on TV. The man's name might have been Lester. It was a long time ago; Walt Frazier still played for the Knicks, and Walt still had all his moves. He drove the lane, twisted, jumped, double-pumped, scored. On defense he danced, sprinted, danced his man—hands fluttering always at the ball, bodies checking bodies, high-tops squeaking up the polished wood floor. Roy mentioned to Lester that he had heard the pros will wear out a new pair of shoes in a single game. Lester said that was true.

Roy had been in a car accident, and his leg was broken in two places. He still has trouble going to his left when he plays basketball in pickup games. Lester didn't have any legs. His legs had been amputated at the knees.

When the Knicks called time-out, Lester told Roy he'd been sleeping in a stolen car the week it snowed so much. Every day Lester got colder, and every day he found it harder to get out of the car. Then he didn't get out for three days. Then somebody found him, even though the car had been parked on the street the whole time. Some kids had taken the hubcaps, then the tires, then the bumper. Frostbite, gangrene, no legs.

"Motherfuckers gonna have to take care of me now," Lester said. "I don't give a shit, though. I still got my dick."

When Anne and Roy were first married, they went to New York. They walked through Central Park in the snow, and Roy showed Anne an apartment building across the street, the Dakota, and he said, "That's where John Lennon lives." Roy told Anne that he and John Lennon had the same birthday. Anne asked Roy if he thought John Lennon was more popular than Jesus and God.

"You mean, are the Beatles more popular?" Roy corrected her, and then he said maybe, and then he wanted to go back to Anne's sister's apartment, where they were staying, because the wind had picked up and Central Park was cold. Roy thought about their chances of getting mugged, and about the car accident he'd had a few years before, and about Walt Frazier retiring from basketball. On the way back they passed the ice-skating rink. Anne wanted to rent skates and try it, but Roy said he was too cold.

Central Park was winter dead again once they were away from the bright lights at the ice-skating rink. The trees looked naked and hard, like they could hurt someone and not know it. Roy thought he and Anne must be the only people alive in the park. Anne said something in German. She told Roy it was a poem—by Goethe, of course—but she wouldn't tell him what it meant. He had to find his own translation.

Over all the hilltops
Silence,
Among all the treetops
You feel hardly
A breath moving.
The birds fall silent in the woods.
Simply wait! Soon
You too will be silent.

It was snowing a year later in New York when that boy shot John Lennon. Roy calls him a boy; the guy couldn't have known what he was doing. He looked so young and so angry in all the pictures. After Sarah was born, Roy told Anne he thought it would be nice if Sarah married John and Yoko's son. "We could arrange the marriage now," Roy told her. "Set it up with Yoko, explain about the birthdays and all, then in twenty years the kids could marry. Just like they do in India and places like that." Anne said, "But we don't even know Yoko."

This morning, Roy, who is obviously not very practical, suggested they get a room in the Holiday Inn until the cold weather passes. "We could bring a hotplate," he told Anne, "and cook in the bathroom. Sarah would be warm. We wouldn't have to worry about drafts and cold walls and frozen pipes." Anne said no, they couldn't afford it. Roy didn't say anything. He tried to turn up the gas heater, but it was already on as high as it could go. After Anne left the house, Roy hauled out the blankets and nails.

Roy's hammering wakes Sarah again, and he knows he's too anxious to deal with her. Sometimes when she cries Roy worries that she won't ever stop, that she'll cry herself sick, and keep crying even then. Maybe he should hang a blanket between the living room and the kitchen—to block the sound. There isn't a door to close. Something a little out of control in Roy wants to shake her to make her stop crying. He's thinking he *has* to get these blankets up—

Roy puts down the hammer.

Never shake a baby in anger or frustration, the pediatrician told Roy and Anne. Roy never has, but he can understand the impulse. A guy Roy knows confessed once in an encounter group for new parents that he had jerked his little boy out of the crib and had shaken him. The baby had been crying nonstop for an hour. No one in the group said anything at first. Then a woman stood up and walked over to the man—they were in a circle on the floor—and she kicked him.

Roy thinks he'll stay away from Sarah for a while. She was up all morning, and he knows she's still tired. She'll go back to sleep if he's quiet, if he stops hammering these blankets to the wall.

It's an hour later. Roy wants a cigarette, but he quit smoking a year ago when Anne got pregnant. Studies show that even second-hand smoke can harm the baby's development, the obstetrician told them. Roy's last pack of Camels, the cellophane unbroken, sits in the back of the closet in the pocket of a coat he never wears. Roy thinks about it a lot, though. He still misses it. They say a smoker is never alone, and Roy can never quite shake the belief that the red ember glowing on the end of a cigarette might be just enough fire sometime to keep him warm.

Anne should be home any time now. Roy's got Sarah in his lap, and she's got her bottle. They're sitting on the floor under the last blanket beside the heater, and he's feeding her and rocking her. The living room, which was never large, seems even smaller with all the blankets nailed to the walls. The plastic over the windows keeps them in that kind of half-night that drives the Scandinavians crazy above the Arctic Circle. Roy has done all he can to make the house warm.

He wishes Sarah were older—just for a minute older, then small again. He thinks he should tell her, before he forgets, about her mother wanting to ice skate one afternoon in Central Park. And maybe Roy should tell her about the man with no legs. Sarah fights with her bottle. "You can't win," Roy says. She needs her diaper changed.

Of course there are other things Roy doesn't want Sarah to know.

He thinks about that boy who shot John Lennon. He thinks about Goethe's "Wanderers Nachtlied." The feeling of winter, to Roy, is the feeling of outrunning your headlights while driving at night. You try to anticipate, but really you end up staring past the headlights into the darkness not so far ahead to the coming of another Ice Age.

# Driver's Ed

Nineteen seventy-two will always be this day.

You're seventeen, you're chasing your girlfriend, but she's outrunning you—something that's never happened before. You stop, and she dances ahead of you through the amber light of the North Carolina pine forest. *Amber* is your word for it, because the afternoon sun through the trees looks just like that rock your pal Larry B. showed you once, the one from Peru with the bug locked inside.

You've been smoking too many cigarettes—that's why you don't want to run. Also, you and Joyce, your girlfriend, just screwed, and you don't like the way the skin rubs the inside of your jeans. *Screwed* is your word, too, though Joyce doesn't care for it. She says things like "You may be screwing, but I'm making love." That's easy for her to say, of course, since she's not the one who's double-rubbering.

You push your hair behind your ears, fan yourself with your T-shirt. The real reason you stopped running is that you've been thinking about stealing Larry B.'s car, and Larry B. is just ahead waiting at the picnic blanket. You're stalling; you don't want to look at

Larry B. You lean against a tree. Joyce doesn't even realize you're not chasing her.

And that's when the dog attacks.

From nowhere, a German shepherd—mean dog—slams Joyce against a tree, leaps up, catches her thigh with his front paws. You see blood. You yell. From twenty yards away you see the shepherd's pink erection as the dog rubs up and down, squeezing Joyce's bare leg. Joyce's eyes go wide with shock. She stares, helpless, at the slobbering dog. You run, but you don't seem to be moving with enough speed or purpose. You feel like a man who can't swim, who stands on the shore and watches somebody drown.

And then big Larry B. appears, as suddenly as the dog. Grabs the shepherd by the hair on his back, drags him off Joyce. The dog rakes his claws down Joyce's leg, leaving thin red lines from her thigh to her knee. Larry B. kicks hard and the dog retreats, barks crazily in circles, then races off through the pines.

Larry B. helps Joyce sit beside the tree—actually guides her as she slides down the sticky bark. He looks up smiling as you approach. It's a broad, fleshy smile that immediately has you thinking again about Larry B.'s car, about secondary roads and driving at night. "Hey B.—," you say. "Portrait of an American hero."

Joyce, crying a little, gives you a look that suggests you're paying attention to the wrong person. You kneel to inspect her wounds, which don't look too serious. You touch her thigh near the cuts and wish you'd been the one to save her.

"That dog," says Larry B. "Maybe he was just looking for friends."

Joyce says "Jesus Christ" under her breath, hisses it the way a mother might if she thought her kid was being stupid. You hate it when she does that. Larry B. rolls his eyes, indicating that he thinks she's maybe overreacting, and you regret inviting Larry B. to join you and Joyce for your picnic. It wears you out trying to stay sensitive to Joyce and B. at the same time.

Larry B. stands up. "Just a flesh wound," he announces.

"I think I can walk okay," Joyce says—bravely, you think. You always admire her when it comes to pain. She handles it so well, maybe even thrives on it sometimes. She had a cyst removed from her ovaries last year. The day after the operation she wanted to go home. The first time you screwed—made love—in the back seat of Joyce's father's baby-blue Lincoln, you knew it hurt her, but she still wouldn't give up.

Your old wrestling coach, Coach Riley, would love someone like Joyce. She should have been the guy, you decide; you should have been the girl. You're not like Joyce; you don't get along very well with pain.

"Coach—" you remember saying more than once, blood creeping from your lip while the side of your face swelled where you'd just been kicked by a wrestling boot—"I've gotta go home." Riley would just smile. "Practice isn't over yet, Mister." He always called the wrestlers "Mister." He said it encouraged them to act like adults. "No pain, no gain, Mister," he would say, as if he was the original guy who coined the phrase. You think he's an asshole.

"News flash." Larry B. makes you jump. "News flash. North Carolina girl attacked by horny dog." He's trying to make you laugh with his radio voice as the three of you shuffle back to the picnic blanket. "Girl says, 'Best I ever had.'"

Joyce blushes angrily, but B. keeps it up. "Dog sales jump in sleepy community. Poodles exchanged for Great Danes. Husbands and boyfriends suffer inferiority complexes." You feel the friendly pat of Larry B.'s hand on the back of your jeans—you know it's just friendly, but you tense up anyway, you think about that car.

Larry B. is a disc jockey on FM radio. His station broadcasts out of a mobile home, but they have the strongest signal in eastern North Carolina north of Camp Lejeune and south of Elizabeth City. "This is WMBB—playing the b-b-best in contemporary radio. And this is the Larry B. show." B. is twenty-five; he's been to college; he's worked in Raleigh. He knows something about the world beyond the rivers that draw their lines around your town, and that's why you've attached yourself to him. And in another month, the day after high school is over, you are supposed to pack everything you own into Larry B.'s red '67 Mustang; you're going to hide your dope stash in the empty water reservoir under the hood, you're going to climb into those vinyl bucket seats, you're going to crank up that smooth, purring engine, and you're going to drive.

Unless you steal the car first.

The car is parked a quarter of a mile away, just off the dirt road, and you and Joyce watch from the picnic blanket as Larry B. fades off into the trees. He's going for the first-aid kit under the front seat, for Merthiolate and gauze pads. It's all Weyerhaeuser Paper Company land here, and all the pines are Weyerhaeuser pines, a fact that depresses you whenever you think about it. You and Joyce have been visiting the pine forest for several months now—it's littered with your condoms—and you don't like the idea of a systematic harvest wiping out all traces that you'd ever been here.

"Well, they really do take good care of their trees," Joyce always points out. "They never cut without planting back, you know."

You take off your T-shirt, thinking about that, thinking about how Joyce doesn't quite get it. You splash some Mogen David wine on your shirt and wipe Joyce's leg. You can tell it stings her from the way she sucks the air in suddenly through her teeth.

"Are you sure this is such a good idea?" she asks, clenching the edge of the blanket.

"It's alcohol," you say. "Alcohol's what you use to clean wounds."

"But is this the same kind of alcohol?"

You take a drink. "Alcohol is alcohol. Kills all kinds of germs, inside and out. Larry B. says—"

"Oh Larry B. Damn Larry B."

"He happens to be a very close personal friend of mine."

"And you happen to be going away with him."

You splash some MD directly on her leg. Joyce hisses.

"That's enough. Don't do that anymore."

Joyce pouts. She doesn't want you to go, but you've been all through this before. You even asked her to come with you once, but she knew you didn't mean it. There is no way you're staying. No way in hell. The town is too small. If you ever get any mail there—not that anybody does—people open it and read it first.

You've heard that from more than one source, and you believe it. It's that kind of town. Your life is not your own.

You got hassled all last fall for quitting the wrestling team; they even scratched it on your locker: "Teammates don't forgive." You still remember the scene when Riley called you into his office. "Son, I know what you're trying to do here—believe me, I understand. You say you don't like to get hurt, but I know better. You think you can prove something by quitting. Maybe to me, maybe to your parents, maybe to your girlfriend—"

"No sir. She doesn't want me to quit, either."

Riley ignored you. "Maybe you don't know who you're trying to prove this something to. But do you know who really suffers? It's your teammates who really suffer. They're like your brothers—they are your brothers—and if you turn your back on them . . . well, I think you understand."

Riley folded his hands in front of him and smiled at you like the army recruiters on television commercials. You fingered the scar that bends around the outside of your eye like a tiny horseshoe; you got that at Regionals. "No," you said. "I just don't want to get hurt anymore, and I don't want to hurt anybody. I'm nonviolent."

"Nonviolent!" Riley exploded. "Nonviolent! Wrestling's not violent, Mister. Wrestling is controlled aggression. Controlled aggression. If you want violence, then play football. If you want to be nonviolent, then give up that sport." Riley rose halfway out of his chair, his red hands gripping the edge of his desktop. "Do you understand that? Wrestling is finely tuned, controlled aggression.

Violence is undisciplined aggression. Wrestling is the essence of physical discipline and control."

You took a step backward because he was spitting as he shouted. "Look, man. I already told you I don't want to wrestle. I'm nonviolent."

"Then I pity you, Mister."

"Hey—don't pity me, man. How about if I pity you? How about that? How about if I pity you, you Nazi?"

That got you suspended for two days, but you didn't care at the time. You did pity Riley, you really did—stuck like he was in your town. Riley grew up there. He wrestled for William & Mary— that was his one great glory—then he came back to teach driver's ed, coach the wrestling team, and date divorcees at the Methodist church. He lived in a fucking trailer.

You, on the other hand, have been nonviolent since last summer when some peace guys in Greenville, collecting for a North Vietnamese children's fund, gave you and Alvin Holloman a lot of antiwar literature. It was at an Allman Brothers concert at the university—before Duane Allman died. Alvin Holloman was tripping at the concert and you tied a rope around his wrist and had to lead the boy around all night while Alvin read passages from the antiwar literature like he was reading from the Bible. The experience changed your life. He kept standing on seats and bothering people who were trying to enjoy the concert; he kept weeping over the brothers and sisters in Hanoi while the Allman Brothers played "Tied to the Whipping Post."

A week later Alvin was tripping again, and he got arrested for trying to hitchhike naked out of your town in the middle of the night. They found him near the bridge. He was already on probation for selling a lid of pot to a junior high school kid, but you were still surprised when they sent Alvin to jail. You didn't know they could send guys to jail if they were seventeen.

"Do you want something to eat?" you ask Joyce. You shuffle through a pile of tapes, trying to choose between Led Zeppelin and Joni Mitchell. Larry B. still isn't back with the first-aid kit, and you wonder for a second if he might not abandon you and Joyce in the pines. You wonder if B. has any idea you're even thinking about taking the Mustang.

"What is there?" Joyce says. She's lying on her back. You know she likes Led Zeppelin, but you're leaning toward Joni Mitchell. Larry B. likes Joni Mitchell.

"Boiled eggs," you say. You fixed the lunch. You plug *For the Roses* into the portable tape player. "Got boiled eggs and donuts. And boiled peanuts." You look through the basket. "And napkins. And some Boone's Farm if you don't like Mogen David. And Dr Pepper for medicinal purposes. Maybe you ought to have some of that."

Joyce sits up, pine straw clinging to her hair. "That's all munchie food."

"No it's not. There's no candy in here."

"Donuts?"

"It's vegetarian food. I'm a vegetarian."

"You're going to be a dead vegetarian if this is all you eat."

Sometimes Joyce sounds just like your mother. "Well, I would have brought cheese sandwiches," you say, "but we only had white bread and processed cheese."

"What's wrong with that? It beats boiled peanuts and Boone's Farm."

"Nobody's saying it's a perfect diet. But it's better than killing animals."

"I read somewhere that scientists recorded tomatoes scream-ing when they were cut by a knife. What about the screaming tomatoes?"

"Look, I don't care if you don't want to eat anything."

Joyce studies the basket of food. "Since when are you a vegetarian?"

"Since Tuesday."

"Four days?"

"Larry B.'s a vegetarian," you say, reluctantly.

Joyce forces one of her phony laughs. "Right. And he weighs two hundred pounds. You want to know why? French fries and pizza. That's all he eats. Are you going on the pizza-and-fries diet, too? Are you going to turn into a Larry B. junior?"

"Larry B.," you start to say for the one millionth time, "is a close personal friend—"

"Oh hell," Joyce says. "Larry B. is queer."

You put down your donut; the white powder sticks to your fingertips, but you can't bring yourself to lick them off. "You shouldn't say things like that, Joyce," you say quietly. "Not about people's friends."

"It's true. Larry B.'s queer."

"How do you know?" You feel your face go hot, and your stomach turns, as if you just ate something bad. You've always known, of course. But—

"Because Johnny Hackey told my brother."

"Johnny Hackey's an asshole. I wouldn't believe anything he said." You suddenly can't stop thinking about Larry B.'s big hands always squeezing your arm or slapping your leg—all just affectionately, just friendly contact. "How would Johnny Hackey know?"

"That party last weekend at T.D.'s farm."

"Where they roasted that pig?"

"A lot of people stayed over. They had a couple of kegs, and T.D. had half a pound of Greenville Green."

"So?"

"Johnny Hackey and Larry B. were going to sleep in the back of somebody's van. Johnny Hackey told my brother that he woke up in the middle of the night, and Larry B.'s hand was you-know-where."

You feel sick. You fold your arms over your bare chest and wish your T-shirt weren't purple wet with Mogen David because you want to put it on. Larry B. queer. Damn. Goddamn.

Joyce says your name softly with her little girl voice, the one she uses when she wants you to ask her if she wants to have sex so she can say yes. "You don't have to go with him, you know. You could still apply to Greenville. I'll be going."

You unscrew the Mogen David cap. "College," you say. "Do you want to know what college is all about?" You're glad to be diverted; you don't want to think about Larry B. You continue.

# untitled

"They had this philosophy test one time in this philosophy class, and all the students opened their test books and there was only one question: 'Why?'"

"Why what?" Joyce says

"Nothing. Just 'Why?'"

"That was the question?"

"Right—'Why?' was the question."

"What was the answer?"

"'Because.' 'Because' was the right answer. 'Why? Because.' Test over. Now what do I need to go to college for to learn that?"

Joyce isn't sold, though. "Where did you get that story, anyway?" She says it as if she already knows the answer, and you decide you probably hate her. You can just see Joyce four years from now with her business degree from college, and her real estate license, selling houses for her daddy to people who don't think they have a choice but to buy. They'll sign on the dotted line and hate Joyce at the same time, because she'll be so transparently sure about what they have to do.

Larry B. queer, you think. Damn. Goddamn.

Joyce is rubbing your foot, sliding her hand inside the leg of your jeans to massage your calf. She says your name again, trying to be seductive, but she just sounds even more like her mother, the way her mother baby-talks her father. You wonder if girls in California all sound like their mothers. You doubt they do. You doubt anybody out there double-rubbers, either. And they probably know better wines to drink than MD 20-20 and Boone's Farm, better vegetarian food than french fries and boiled peanuts, better things to do with their lives than go to college for four years and then come home to work for their fathers or teach driver's ed or plant trees for Weyerhaeuser to mow down.

And then, of course, there's the draft. You'll be eighteen this summer; you'll be in the next lottery. But they don't draft guys from California. It's an East Coast war is what you've heard.

You see yourself driving alone in B.'s Mustang, fingers curled around the wheel, cruising through the desert at night. Isn't there a desert between your town and California? Where the hell is Death Valley? You know you've seen it on TV.

Joyce rubs a little higher on your leg, lightly brushing the soft skin behind your knee with her fingertips. "You don't even know what you're giving up yet," she says softly, and this time the softness surprises you. "And what about me?" You roll closer so she can keep touching you until you hear Larry B.'s shuffling footsteps approaching through the pines. Joni Mitchell is singing a song called "Electricity."

When Larry B. returns with the Merthiolate he says he saw the dog again near the dirt road where the car is parked. "I gave him your phone number," B. says to Joyce. Joyce says she doesn't think that's too funny, and you stop coloring her leg with Merthiolate and suggest you all eat. Larry B. isn't thrilled about the picnic food either, although he eats a couple of donuts and drinks a Dr Pepper. Joyce asks him if he'd rather have some french fries, but B. ignores her. You watch him carefully for any signs that maybe she hurt his feelings, but you can't detect any. Larry B. is a pretty sensitive guy.

You say you're sorry that you didn't pack anything good to eat, and B. smiles and tells you not to worry about it. You know perfectly well why the smile makes you uncomfortable, but you don't know what to do about it. Larry B. queer. OK. So? Larry B. squeezes your shoulder, and you pretend that you have to move away to straighten a corner of the blanket—out of the range of B.'s friendly hands. Joyce keeps giving you profound looks, as if every gesture is proof that B. is what she says he is, until finally you can't stand it. There's no sun slanting through the pines anymore, although it's still light. You pull on your wet T-shirt, which sucks to your skin where it's still wet from the wine.

"Munchie food," you say, and you slap the basket lid shut. "So maybe if we got stoned it would taste better. Did you bring the dope, B.?"

Larry B. spits soggy peanut shells into his fist. "Left it in the car."

"Want me to go get it?" you ask. "Want to get stoned?"

"Sure," Larry B. says. "Whatever you want to do."

Joyce looks at you—suspiciously, maybe—but you don't wait for her to say anything. You grab the keys from Larry B. and try not to run away from them both. Joni Mitchell is singing "You Turn Me On, I'm a Radio," and the song chases you through the pines the way TV commercial jingles always follow you to the kitchen when you leave the living room to get something to eat.

As you hurry through the shaded alley between two rows of pines, you think again about taking Larry B.'s car. Here's your chance and you know it. Joyce and B. wouldn't be able to get to a phone for hours. You cashed a couple of savings bonds last week, and that with everything else you've saved gives you not quite two hundred dollars. Would two hundred dollars get you to California? How long could you live on two hundred dollars? Where would you stay? You can't remember ever being any farther west in your life than Tennessee. Your family went to Canada once for a vacation—really just over the border at Niagara Falls. The idea of stealing Larry B.'s car and driving it alone out to California suddenly seems about as likely, and as terminal, as riding a barrel over Niagara Falls. Was it the fall that killed all those guys, or did they drown in the river—pushed down and kept under by the crush of the water?

You remember a story about a couple of men on a barge that broke loose on the Niagara River. The barge floated down almost to the Falls and got hung up on some rocks in the middle of the churning water, so close that the spray poured on the guys all night like rain while they waited for daylight and their rescue. Only when the rescuers reached the barge the next morning all they found were two dead men, their hair turned white from some sort of chemical change triggered by their fear. And it was the fear that killed them. It was the hair, though, that always made you queasy. One day just normal guys with friends and families and brown hair or black hair or blond hair, any color hair. And the next day—

Well it's a stupid story, you decide. For one thing, nobody's hair is going to turn white unless they get old. And even then most people would just dye it. And for another thing, you don't believe anybody was ever that helpless as to get stuck on a loose barge waiting for Niagara Falls to kill them. That's just one of those stories they tell little kids to keep them in line, do what they're told, that sort of thing.

You come to the dirt road, and it's like stepping out of a dark room. The pine forest suddenly seems gloomy now that you're out of it, and Larry B.'s Mustang sits waiting for you fifty yards up the road. As you walk to the car, jangling the keys against your leg, you see a brown shape appear from the pines—just for a second—and then vanish farther up the road. You feel that panic that used to grab your throat just before a wrestling match—the fear not only that you were going to lose but that you were going to get pinned in the first takedown, cry right there on the mat, embarrass yourself and your team and your coach and your family. You unlock the door quickly and jump in on the driver's side. You aren't sure why the dog frightens you so much; you've never been afraid of dogs. Maybe it has rabies. That might explain why the dog attacked Joyce. More than likely, though, he smelled the sex. You try to remember all you know about rabies, but you can't come up with much. Isn't it with rabies that the cure can kill you, too? Don't they give you shots in the stomach? If you'd never seen *Old Yeller* you doubt you'd even know what rabies is.

And that's the damn problem: you just don't know enough. That's why everything's so hard. With the exception of Larry B., none of your friends seems to know very much either, even guys who went to Greenville or to State or to Chapel Hill. They come home, and they know a lot of good beer-drinking games. And hell, you hardly have any friends left, now that you think about it—none of the old crowd, anyway. Your jock buddies deserted you in the fall; or maybe you deserted them. Alvin Holloman is in jail, and he was fried from too many drugs before that. Chris Daughtry turned into a Jesus freak, and any time you try to talk to Chris he pulls out his New Testament. Daughtry was the guy who first got you stoned. You worked together last summer at Kentucky Fried Chicken, and Daughtry was a crazy man then. He once went a week eating nothing but chicken gizzards and livers just to win a five dollar bet. Then he took the five and bought another bucket of gizzards. Now he's as pious as the front row families at church.

And Donnie Parker. Donnie Parker is just gone. No one knows where—not even his parents. The rumor is that he stole a Harley Davidson Sportster from a junkie in Raleigh who owed him some money. Donnie got busted with a quarter pound just before Christmas; he disappeared in March the week before his court date. Some people say he stole the Sportster and rode it down to Florida to sell, which might be true, since he used to live down there.

You rest your hands on the steering wheel at ten and two—just like Riley taught you in driver's ed. At least you learned something from the coach. You think about a line from another Joni Mitchell song that lays out the limited options for what people have to turn to these days: Jesus, heroin, or rambling around. It seems to fit the situation, but you also have this sudden fear that all the truth you'll ever know in your life will come from lines in songs like that.

You slide the key into the ignition and pinch it around with your thumb and forefinger. The engine turns over, pistons move, cylinders fire, there isn't a hitch in the rhythm. You pull the seat up, put your hands on the wheel again and brace yourself in. You close your eyes and feel the smooth vibration spread from under the hood. It's easy to imagine the motion. Out of the pine forest, north toward Elizabeth City, not even stopping to pack. Past Elizabeth City. To hell with Elizabeth City. To hell with Carolina. You have a cousin in Richmond who could help you sell the Mustang. You would hate to part with such a good car, but you could do plenty with the money. Take a bus to California. Yeah. Only what will you do when you get there? Who do you know out there? What happens next?

You drop a hand off the wheel and touch an eight-track tape that sits in Larry B.'s tape deck. It's the Rolling Stones. Funny how a guy like Larry B. can like the Stones and also like Joni Mitchell so much. You guess that if you're a disc jockey you have to like all kinds of music. You can't be particular.

A noise outside the car surprises you, and you look up anxiously, expecting to see the German shepherd. Instead you see Larry B. emerging from the pine forest, as if your thoughts have magically brought him here. You're embarrassed to be caught with the engine running, and you roll down the window—nonchalantly you hope—and you lean on your elbow against the door.

"I don't know what got into me, B. I just felt like starting the car."

Larry B. shrugs. "Everything OK?"

"Yeah, sure. Runs like a dream." You plug in the Stones tape, not sure what else to do. You wonder if it's such a good idea leaving

Joyce alone, with the dog still around, but you don't say anything.

"It's gonna be great, isn't it?" B. asks, not really looking at you, staring over the roof of the car at something up the road.

Then Larry B. looks down. "We're still going to go, aren't we? You still want to travel?"

You put your hands back on the wheel at ten and two. "Hey, yeah," you say. You roll your fingers over the grooves down the back of the steering wheel until your hands rest together at the bottom. "We can go a lot of great places in a car like this."

You look away from B., look up the road twenty yards, and you're not surprised at all when you find yourself looking into the red eyes of the German shepherd. The shepherd sits stone still— mouth open, tongue out—and you could swear the dog is staring back at you, staring and even grinning, with those blood red eyes, the terrible Boy Scout motto:

Be prepared.

# Camouflage

The minute they heard about the gunman, the principal got on the intercom and ordered the teachers to lock the doors, close the blinds, and hide the children under their desks. Maggie Moon, in kindergarten, told her dad later that was how she got the gum in her hair—from under a desk, and it was still soft so some kid must have chewed it on the way to school and left it just that morning. The gunman pounded on the cafeteria door—as if anyone would open it, just like that, and let him in—but the cafeteria workers had barricaded themselves in with the long, low tables. The school-breakfast kids were shivering in the produce locker long after the pounding stopped. Everybody heard the police sirens—finally, thank god—but doors stayed bolted until the principal got back on the intercom and said it was OK, the gunman was gone, last seen tearing through the woods across the street from the school. Police speculated that he had a car waiting at the Park 'n' Shop half a mile away on Route 1. He was wearing camouflage, but nobody reported anything suspicious over there.

   Jeff Moon heard all about it on the radio that afternoon while he was still at work, and he left the office right away. He didn't want his daughter riding the bus home when school let out because there was no telling if the gunman might be hiding somewhere, waiting to ambush. The police didn't seem to have a clue. Jeff Moon only got as far as the Park 'n' Shop, though, and had to abandon his car because traffic was backed up so badly from the school. The radio report had apparently triggered a mass hysteria, and stalled parents were stabbing out their frustrations on their car horns. One was programmed to toot "Yellow Rose of Texas"—not what you'd expect in Virginia—and it looped over and over behind him as Jeff Moon hiked the shortcut up into the same dark woods the gunman had run through earlier. He prayed there was no police stakeout that might mistake him for the gunman, coming back to the scene of the crime.

At the principal's office he wedged into line behind a woman with long, wet hair dripping down onto her VIRGINIA IS FOR LOVERS sweatshirt, and he realized he could read what the shirt said because she had it on backward. She must have come straight from the shower, and she was crying.

"They should have called us," the woman said to someone farther up in line. "They're required to notify us when this happens. They should have sent the children home."

"We'll go to the school board," a voice said back. "We have parents' rights."

Jeff Moon wondered about that—about parents' rights—but he had never seen a list or anything, and he had no idea what they might be. Probably parents didn't have rights. Probably they signed them away as absently as they signed their checks for the school lunches. He thought he should call his wife, Dusty, who was in therapy that afternoon with her agoraphobia group. There was no telling how she would react to news of the gunman, so maybe she should hear it from him. But then a rush of agitated parents through the school doors pushed everyone together, and the line dissolved into a surging mob that percolated toward the principal's office. Jeff Moon was jammed so close to the woman with wet hair that he could smell her shampoo.

"Quiet please," the principal shouted, somewhere ahead. "Everybody quiet please," and Jeff thought about that old spelling device, "The principal is your pal." This principal, whose name was Marriott, kept shouting, "Quiet please. Everybody quiet please," but none of them listened. They demanded their children. They wanted to know which classroom. They were crazy for directions.

"I'm glad you came and got me," Maggie Moon said fifteen minutes later, as she and her dad picked their way past broken glass in the woods behind the Park 'n' Shop. They had to detour around an old mattress, green from age and exposure, that someone had dragged into the brush. Jeff Moon slapped a Thunderbird bottle with the side of his boot, then ducked a condom drooping from a gray branch.

"Were you scared?" he asked.

"No. I didn't want to ride the bus. The bus driver won't let us talk anymore. She yelled at that boy Michael."

Her dad asked if she knew what had happened at her school that morning, and Maggie said they had a drill, but when he asked if she knew why, she said no.

"What do you do in a drill?" he asked.

"Get under your desk."

"And that's how you got the gum?"

Maggie Moon started to cry. "I don't like my school anymore."

"Why?"

"If you're bad you get your name on the board. And if you're bad again you get a check. And then you can't be a Good Apple at the end of the week. And there's gum under the desks. And the teacher yells at you when you have drills. Everybody yells at you."

Jeff wanted to say something to comfort her—"Maybe they were just upset about other things"—but the thought seized him that since the gunman had eluded the police he might still be in these woods, hidden under leaves, waiting in his camouflage for someone foolish and vulnerable and alone. He picked Maggie up and ran the rest of the way back to the Park 'n' Shop.

At home, Maggie went to her room, and when her dad checked on her later she was playing with She-Ra dolls. The She-Ras were women warriors, a present from her mother. They had swords and shields and a pink castle on hinges that opened up if she wanted to spread things out or closed into a handy storage box. Maggie pretended the She-Ras were babies, and she lined them up under a blanket.

Jeff Moon called his office, Triangle Adjusters ("Service, Quality,

Pride"). He hoped there wouldn't be any messages, but there were. A groundskeeper at Massaponax Mills had lost half his hand in a mower accident. Those four chemical workers from the chlorine spill last month in Dumfries had found a quack ophthalmologist willing to testify to permanent vision damage. And Dusty was on a field trip with her agoraphobia group.

She came home an hour later with a gun.

"I heard everything on the radio," she said before she sat down. "Your office told me you had already gone to pick her up."

"So you went to a gun store?"

"We voted. It was where we wanted to go."

Jeff took a minute to think about this. Once, maybe a year ago, before she got help, Dusty crawled under the bed to retrieve one of Maggie's dolls, and she stayed there for an entire afternoon. When Jeff got home that day she was still there, but he found Maggie first—she was in the living room asleep under all the cushions on the couch—and he worried that what Dusty had might be hereditary. The therapy group's initial meetings had been conference phone calls because nobody would leave their homes, and they had only recently started taking short walks together from the office as part of their systematic desensitization. But now . . .

"A gun, Dusty? You're going to escort the bus? Patrol the school? This doesn't make sense."

"I think it makes sense to me," Dusty said, not looking at him, but weighing the pistol in her hand, fingers open, offering it to her husband.

"But we believe in gun control."

"You do—," she started. "You believe that. I believe in life control."

Jeff said that sounded like something her therapist might teach them to say in the agoraphobia group. Dusty said so what if it was— the truth was the truth whether he believed it or not. He thought that sounded like a therapy line, too, but he didn't say anything. Dusty brushed her red hair from her face, using the crook of the arm that held the pistol, and Jeff plucked the gun from her hand.

"It's a Beretta," she said, patting her jeans pocket for Jeff didn't know what: a receipt, change, a cigarette. Then, in a voice he hadn't heard before, she told him it was a .25 caliber automatic, it held a seven-shot clip, and it had a nickel-plated barrel. The handle was walnut.

"Walnut," he repeated. The word didn't seem to belong in this conversation.

"The salesman called it a girl's gun. He said girls like the nickel plating because it's pretty, when really it's just cheaper."

Jeff asked, sarcastically, how she could resist a pitch like that.

"I decided I *wanted* a girl's gun. It fit perfectly in my hand— like a hairbrush. Or like a hammer." Dusty took the gun back and pointed it at Jeff's feet. She said, "Bang," then she said "Dance, Mister." It was supposed to be a joke, but she didn't smile in the right place. Jeff said he didn't think it was very funny.

Dusty went upstairs—to check on Maggie, she said—and Jeff wondered what the two of them would talk about alone. He thought maybe they had a different language when he wasn't around or when they assumed he wasn't around—something barely verbal, like signing—but he hadn't decided yet whether that was a liability or a bond.

The phone rang, and it was his office calling about a cave-in in Stafford, where Triple-D Construction was cutting foundation for an office building. They needed him to do the on-site. He wrote a note for Dusty, not wanting to disturb whatever she and Maggie were talking about upstairs, then left for the accident site. He heard a faint buzz in his head the whole time he was gone, as if something had clotted at the base of his skull and the noise emanated from there. He couldn't shake the sensation that today was fated, that it was bad to be outside. He kept a lookout for snipers.

The world Jeff Moon knew was a more reasonable place, a more secure place than Dusty's. At work with his actuarial tables, he could see what was what—the cost of a hand, an eye, a foundation. Depending on the policy. He knew, too, that every action had its consequences. Two fender benders and you could bet on a rate hike, or, once you factored in the severity, cancellation. There was a connection here—though Jeff couldn't articulate it very well—with a story he had read once when he was a kid, sitting in a doctor's waiting room. Maybe it was *Life* magazine, because he remembered pictures. The article was about a boy who lost his arm, torn clean off his shoulder when he hopped onto the side of a moving train but then smacked into the edge of a tunnel. Luckily the arm stayed put in the sleeve of the boy's jacket, and doctors miraculously reattached it—the first operation of its kind. Everything worked perfectly. The boy could still play Little League even. The story was awful—hop a train, lose an arm. Yet it was tidy—hold on, we can fix this.

Dusty saw things differently. Literally. When Jeff and Dusty first met, she was painting miniature landscapes with brushes so fine he wouldn't touch them for fear they would break. She rarely used a magnifying glass, which was a standard tool for most miniaturists, because she said her eyes were that sharp—like Ted Williams, who could see the seams turn on a baseball coming at him ninety miles an hour from the pitcher's mound. She stopped painting when she got agoraphobia or when she was diagnosed, but she still complained about seeing things that others didn't: certain lights and certain colors, particles in air, shapes in ice.

That night before he put Maggie to bed, Jeff Moon called his brother in Florida to tell him what had happened at the school. Duane interrupted immediately, though, and Jeff couldn't tell if he was trying to be funny or what, like one of the Marx brothers.

"You think you've got gunmen," Duane said. "We had one here at the elementary, he walked right into the cafeteria and actually shot a guy, there where the kids were."

"Did he kill him?"

"Yeah. Shot him in the head."

"Did he know him?"

"Who?"

"Did the gunman know the guy he shot?"

"Oh, yeah," Duane said. "They were both maintenance workers."

"Ours was a stranger."

"Oh." Duane was finally sympathetic. "That's tough, that stranger danger."

When he got off the phone, Jeff saw that Dusty had taken her gun apart and lined up the pieces neatly on newspaper on the living room floor. She had a white handkerchief, a box of Q-tips, and a small jar of oil for cleaning the Beretta. He squatted behind her and touched her shoulders, intending to kiss the back of her head.

She jerked away.

"What?" she said sharply. "What? Don't sneak up like that."

Jeff protested—he wasn't sneaking; it was just affection—but she cut him off and said she was trying to develop new security patterns here and could he please try to be supportive. She was right, of course. Whatever helped—making conference calls with therapy strangers, taking trips to the gun store, being assertive with greasy salesmen—the therapist said she should do. He left her in the living room so he could go upstairs to put Maggie to bed.

But Maggie didn't want to go to bed. She wanted a drink of water, then a different nightgown. Then she wanted a Bobo story. Jeff tried to talk her out of it—he was tired; it was late; he couldn't think of a Bobo story—but she reminded him that he had promised earlier.

He killed the overhead light, felt his way back to her in the dark before his eyes had time to adjust, pulled a quilt over both of them on Maggie's narrow bed. Hall light cast faint geometric shapes in the room, and the She-Ra dolls, lined against the wall like sentries, cast slant shadows that bled together in the corner.

Maggie inched in tight against her dad. Jeff thought he could hear Dusty downstairs cleaning her gun, and he imagined her lost in it the way she once lost herself in the minutiae of her painting. He pictured her surrounded by tiny pins and springs and rods and plates, with the pile growing ominously, like the fishes and the loaves.

"Tell it, Daddy," Maggie said. She pinched softly and held the fleshy inside part of his arm. He touched her hair and began the story—about Bobo and a tiny girl from outer space. Bobo was a giant gorilla, strong, soft-headed, funny. The tiny girl was lost on Earth in her spaceship. One thing happened—some dogs chased her up a tree—then another thing happened—a big wind blew her into the river—before Bobo rescued her and they became friends. The tiny girl missed her family, though, and wanted to go back to her own planet, so Bobo climbed a high mountain and hurled her little ship back into outer space in a perfect trajectory home.

Maggie waited for more, but when it didn't come she started to cry. She said the story made her sad. Also it was too short, and she wouldn't go to sleep until he told her another.

"No more stories," Jeff said. "It's late. It's go-to-sleep time."

She burrowed into the quilt away from him, and he strained to hear Dusty in the living room. He thought he smelled smoke from a cigarette and wondered if he should go downstairs so they could talk about this gun. She knew the statistics, damnit—that you're more likely to shoot a family member than an intruder. He would buy her an attack dog if she thought she needed protection. A rott-weiler. A pit bull.

He eased out of the bed, patted the lump of covers where Maggie's head should have been, and told her to stay. She growled to let him know she wasn't crying now, she was just mad, and then he left her room. He held the rail tightly all the way downstairs as if he were pulling himself under water.

Dusty was sitting cross-legged on the floor in the middle of the living room with the reassembled Beretta. She cradled it with both hands, like a book, eyes fixed on the gun as if she were reading it. She held a cigarette, too, wedged like an accessory between two knuckles. Jeff waited, thinking at any minute she would move the cigarette to her lips and let it hang there while she lifted the gun police-style, squinted over the barrel, and pulled the trigger.

But nothing happened. She sat. She read the gun. The cigarette burned down.

He must have made a noise then, standing at the bottom of the stairs. Hearing him, seeing him, she blushed and hid the pistol under her leg. "It's not loaded," she said. "I haven't loaded it yet. I might not—"

She would have said more, but he couldn't stay. She even called out—"Jeffrey, wait"—but he was already swimming back to the stairs, back to Maggie's room, back to her bed, holding his breath until his lungs burned. The buzzing sound that had haunted him earlier started up again from the base of his skull, and he tried to brace himself against it and against whatever might come next.

"Please another story?" Maggie's muffled voice found an air shaft out of the quilt. She could have been under water too, speaking in bubbles. When he didn't answer right away, she peeked up from the covers.

"Please another?"

Jeff Moon thought hard, but nothing came. He knew the Bobo story had been short; he knew he'd probably told it, or versions of it, a dozen times in the past. He wanted to apologize, explain to Maggie that he didn't have the imagination it took to spin these things off the way some parents did, and he had to borrow from the detritus of his own childhood—shards from kid books, slices from thirty-five-cent matinees—to give them any life at all.

He closed then opened his eyes, and only then realized how dark the room had gotten. The hall light wasn't on anymore—either it had burned out or Dusty had turned it off from downstairs—and there were no shadows on the wall for definition. The She-Ra dolls seemed shrunken, smaller, as if hiding from their posts as sentries.

"Please, Daddy?" Maggie said, but he didn't know any other stories. He was sure he heard Dusty now in the living room, locking the door, closing the blinds, moving furniture. Doing all she could to make them safe for this one night. He wondered how late it was, and he said *Tomorrow, Maggie*—he would tell her the rest tomorrow, there was too much to tell her tonight, and if she rolled over on her stomach he would rub her back for a while. He would draw pictures on her back. "You need to go to sleep," he said. "Please go to sleep," he whispered, and he blindfolded her eyes with one of his hands.

# My Chaos Theory

1. Everything happens for a reason. That's what Reverend Mann told my mom and what my mom told me. Everything. What I said to my mom was I wouldn't be going to her church anymore if I had to listen to stuff like that, and then I rode my bike out to Montford Metals again to see my dad's truck. What looked like blood from a distance turned out to be rust, and the closer I got the less it seemed to be my dad's truck than just another wreck, but I still studied it a long time, trying to figure out all the ways it might have gotten so twisted and smashed, what must have hit what, the exact point of the collision. For some reason the more I stared at it that day, the more I kept thinking not about what happened to my dad but about the time I broke my arm when he pushed me too hard on a tire swing when I was a real little guy and I had what the doctors called a green-stem break. At the hospital they laid me on a table and turned my arm up so they could stick all my fingers in steel-mesh finger-gloves hanging from a rack, so it was like I was raising my hand in class to answer a question, only every one of my fingers was caught in one side of some Chinese handcuffs. My dad stood at my head and said, "Hold on now, this'll only hurt a second,"

but before I could ask him "What?" the doctors wrenched my arm into place, and you could hear the bone grinding back around, and the way my dad leaned all his weight on my shoulders to hold me down plus the way my fingers were locked in those Chinese handcuffs I couldn't move, only my mouth was open but there wasn't any sound, and my eyes got so wide I couldn't see a thing but the light and the outline of my dad.

2. Here's how much I hate Kerry Boss: They say God is love. That's how much. As much as God is love I hate Kerry Boss, and I laughed harder than anybody when he did the stupid things he did, like when he tied the string around his dick and couldn't get it off. Who knows why? Maybe somebody just said one day, "Hey Kerry, bet you wouldn't tie this string around your dick and leave it there," so he did, and he waited a couple of hours before he tried to get it off, but of course by then his dick swelled up and by the next day the head turned purple and he had to tell his dad and they took him to the hospital for a surgeon to cut the string with a scalpel.

We were at Kevin O'Neal's house playing football when we heard about it, and not from Kerry Boss, either, who hid his face in shame for about a week. But word got out. Word always got out. And we laughed so hard that Junior Delillo, the Boy-Who-Had-No-Penis, couldn't control himself and peed down his catheter tube and it got all over his shoe at the bottom of his jeans that he always wore because his mother didn't want anybody to see the tube and the pouch that must have busted because it would embarrass him. Junior Delillo jumped up from the pile of us and ran behind Kevin

O'Neal's house and wouldn't come out until somebody went to get his mom. We liked Junior Delillo OK, though, not like Kerry Boss, so nobody teased him, and of course he couldn't help being born with birth defects, either, and he was deaf, too. Maybe it was from drugs his parents did when they were young that caused chromosome damage. Or maybe his dad hurt his mom when she was pregnant, which is what they say happened to Stevie Espenship's mother and was the thing that gave Stevie Espenship his brain damage. There were a lot of kids with a lot of problems in our neighborhood, I guess. But at least Junior Delillo didn't tie a string around his dick. He just didn't have one was all. And he played football with us and did what we told him as long as we talked slow and he could read our lips.

But Kerry Boss—he was the one always screwing around with you, getting you into the kinds of trouble you ought to see coming at you like a big, slow train you should be able to avoid in your sleep, step off the track, get out of the way, but for some stupid reason you can't, you're stuck like the deer my dad used to freeze in fields at night with his headlights until he got caught and they temporarily took his truck, or like the other time in junior high when Kerry Boss thought he was being cool and smashed my cafeteria roll into my green peas so of course I did the same thing to his lunch tray but one of the cafeteria ladies saw us and turned us in to Mr. Ward and we had to go to his office and listen to his Board of Education speech. Except that time it wasn't a speech, it was for real: he had me first grab the edge of his big wood desk and bend over and he beat me until his arm got tired but I didn't cry—I wouldn't give him or Kerry Boss the satisfaction—I just thought about how hungry I was going to be the rest of the afternoon because I loved those cafeteria rolls and the one Kerry Boss smashed into the peas was about all I was going to eat from the gag-you lunch that day.

Kerry Boss, though, that candy-ass cried the first time Mr. Ward hit him, and I told anybody who would listen to me and anybody else besides. But he was in the neighborhood. He was around. So of course no matter what he did he always got back into things, always got back into the football games at Kevin O'Neal's, always got us into more of the kind of trouble where we were caught without an alibi, put on restrictions, confined to our rooms, shaking our heads and trying to figure out if it was possible we were as dumb as it must seem to have let Kerry Boss screw things up for us like that again and again and again and again.

3. My mother took me to Reverend Mann a couple of times to talk about my bad temper, only Reverend Mann didn't say "bad temper," he said "hostility," like it was a disease. I asked him if he knew Kerry Boss, because if he did he would understand why every kid in the neighborhood had the same disease of hostility—because Kerry Boss was everybody's bad half, he was what got you into trouble. Reverend Mann nodded his head, then said, "Paul, I'd like to hear more about your fight with Stevie Espenship." As if just like that he forgot we were talking about Kerry Boss. As if I hadn't explained it a hundred times already. As if it didn't make the back of my head start hurting all over again to even think about Stevie. And as if I didn't know that no matter what I started talking about—

even the fight—Reverend Mann would eventually try to get me to talk about my dad, who I'd just as soon leave alone if it's all the same to anybody.

"What would your father have said, Paul? Would he have let the other boys goad you into a fight with Stevie Espenship?"

I stared at Reverend Mann's shoes and thought he had the biggest feet I'd ever seen, and he wasn't all that tall either. What I wanted to say, but didn't, was that Yeah, probably my dad would let them goad me into the fight, but if Reverend Mann would give me my dad's phone number I would just call and ask him myself what I was supposed to have done different in the Stevie Espenship situation. News flash: that was last year. Double news flash: I don't want to talk about it anymore.

The Stevie Espenship fight: we were riding bikes after school— me and Kevin O'Neal and Pud Attaway and David Calder and Junior Delillo and Kerry Boss. And we were sitting on our bikes in the middle of the road on Stevie Espenship's street, talking about football, probably—all of those guys with America's Team and me for the Raiders. A door banged open and Stevie came out of his house, and he was out in the street with us before we could split. Old Stevie with his checkered shirt that was too small but buttoned up to his neck. Old Stevie who was the same age and about the same size as us except for his head. Who knows why he chose me? My bike was closest. He liked the color of my math book in the basket. He thought I smelled like cafeteria rolls. Who knows? He grabbed my handlebars. He said something and everybody laughed because he was so hard to understand and when he talked it was like he had to get way high in his throat to get the sound out on top of his breathing so most of it came out his nose. A lot of the words ran together.

Kevin O'Neal said, "What Stevie? What Stevie? What Stevie?" over and over, to freak him out, but Stevie smiled big to get the attention. He said his thing again and everybody kept laughing and it was a whole chorus of the "What Stevies." I pushed at his knuckles to make him let go of my handlebars, but he gripped tighter while they kept up the "What Stevies," then Kerry Boss said, "Why don't you make him let go, Paul? I'd make him let go. I wouldn't let any Bubble Boy jerk my bike around like that." Everybody else said yeah, but then it was right back to the "What Stevies." I shook the handlebars but Stevie still wouldn't let go, and Kerry Boss said, "Oh, I'm sorry. I didn't realize Stevie Espenship was your boyfriend," which would have been too stupid for me to say anything back to except that Kevin O'Neal, who was supposed to be my friend, said, "I guess he loves him."

I turned to Kevin: "He who? Him who?"

Pud Attaway said, "Come on, let's get out of here," and Kerry Boss said, "We'll leave Paul with his homo boyfriend Stevie Espenship," and I got sweaty and flush all of a sudden and got off my bike, only this time I grabbed Stevie's wrist and twisted the skin until I knew it burned, and he finally let go, then I jumped back on my bike. Stevie wasn't through, though, because he grabbed my handlebars again and he spit on my shirt. I guess Kerry Boss must have said some more stupid things then, but I wasn't particularly listening to him so much as I was to that roaring sound like a semi-truck going through my head, and then I threw my bike down and jumped on Stevie.

It wasn't much of a contest. I got him on the ground pretty quick and sat on him. Probably I hit him a couple of times in the chest because I didn't want to mess up his face, but then I just pinned his arms down and really started yelling at him and cussing. When I got done with that I looked up—the truck sound had passed on out of my head by then—and there was Kevin shaking his head and saying, "Jesus, Paul." Stevie Espenship's eyes were as big as mine must have been that day they straightened the green-stem break and I thought the capillaries would bust in Stevie's eyes if he didn't let up soon, and then I started thinking about how bad this would look and what my dad would say when he found out, but then I remembered he wouldn't find out, only my mom would, and she didn't know what to do about anything anymore except have me talk to Reverend Mann. Too late I thought about what my dad would have told me, one of those big lessons I was supposed to learn from him on the cold, boring days we used to sit out on deer platforms waiting to shoot something: that the one thing you don't ever do in a fight is think about it, which was what I was doing, and as soon as I thought that and thought everybody would hate me for beating up a retarded kid, Stevie Espenship got us turned over and next thing I knew he was on top of me with his one hand on my face and the other one grabbing my hair and he was hammering my head against the pavement, and then he stopped that and started slapping my face hard but I was too dazed to make him stop but not too far gone into the concussion they said later at the doctor's that I had that I couldn't see the looks on everybody's faces then—shock and disgust and embarrassment, except for Kerry Boss laughing, and Junior Delillo the only one finally coming over to wrestle Stevie Espenship off of me and send him running on back to his house.

4. For the longest time my dad wouldn't let me shoot, he just had me sit by him on the deer platform and told me not to complain, no matter how cold it got, because that was how his dad had taught him about the woods and about hunting, but none of it seemed to soak in to me the way it did for him because all I could ever think about was going home and watching cartoons. It was about the only time he did spend with me except for when he broke my arm on the swing, and my mom always got excited when we drove off together, me and my dad and his deer rifle, to Alabama to some land some cousins of his owned and let him and me hunt. There was a cabin, too, with a little TV that got bad reception, but at least at night you could watch some shows if the weather wasn't too bad, and you could wrap yourself up in all the blankets and sleeping bags we had and try to ignore the cold wind that came up under the door and through the cracks around the windows where the house had settled crooked because there was no foundation, and the window frames no longer fit right. He drank his beer and we ate out of cans and he tried to teach me stuff about hunting. He might be funny for a little while then, and he might give me some of my own beer in a cup, but usually he just fell asleep and I stayed up alone with the TV.

Once after we'd been on the platform for about half the day he left me with his rifle and said he would be back, and I wasn't to shoot unless I could absolutely tell it was a buck. He hadn't taken a shot all day and I knew he was pissed off about it, but I guess I was pissed off too that he made me stay up there all that time until I couldn't feel my toes, and the gray sky made me depressed thinking I could have been home at Kevin O'Neal's at least playing football, so for no good reason I took a shot at a tree not too long after my dad left. He came running back, even madder that I'd got a shot when he hadn't, but excited too, thinking I might have killed something, but there was nothing and I said I must have missed. He scowled at me and said "Come on" and pretty soon we were walking on the dirt road under the power lines, him with the gun, me with the knapsack with what was left of our sandwiches, and all his crushed cans, and that was when the funny thing happened, which was that we saw a doe and her fawn, right there in the middle of the road in front of us.

The doe started, ears up, eyes as wide as two faces, and bolted to the trees. But the fawn didn't follow. "Why didn't you shoot that deer?" I asked my dad, and he said it was like he already told me, you couldn't shoot a doe right then, and you'd lose your hunting license if you did and got caught. Neither one of us had taken our eyes off the fawn, and what happened next was almost too fast to remember. The fawn just came at us, not bounding but stepping fast and all the time we kept waiting for him to bolt into the trees too with his mother but he didn't. He lowered his head instead and kept coming, veering toward my dad who tried to step out of the way. My dad wasn't quick enough, though, and the fawn butted him in the thigh. My dad did a kind of dance again to try to get away, but the fawn kept it up with his little head—kept butting my dad, and I laughed so hard I rolled in the road on top of the sandwiches, and the fawn kept butting my dad back and back up the road and I never saw anybody dance like my dad did and I almost thought he was doing it for me it was so crazy.

5. I had this science teacher, Mr. Wells. It was his first year and he was way too smart for the school and none of us understood him much. In his classroom he kept a picture on one wall of a guy folded into a wheelchair, a guy worse off than Junior Delillo or even Stevie Espenship, but also a bigger genius than Einstein. Except for being a genius I figured the guy would fit right into our neighborhood, as many problems as he had. Mr. Wells smoked in the classroom, which was against school policy, and mostly he had us sit at our desks and read our science books because he was convinced that none of us read at home. On his other wall he had a map, or actually about twenty sheets of paper taped end to end but not lined up exactly because on it he had plotted a crooked mile of a stream in Colorado that was his graduate school research project. I liked to look at it, even though I didn't understand the symbols, but of course you could tell it was some kind of river. Mr. Wells told me a lot of the time he was plotting he had to climb out on tree limbs over the creek because he had to be careful not to disturb a thing, not a rock, not an inch of soil on the bank, not a single stick, because his purpose was to account for how every

aspect of the creek affected every other aspect of the creek, and the
deeper he got into plotting depth and width and level and obstructions and variations in the shape of the bed, the more there was for
him to account for and the more maddening the project became.
He talked about that river like it was somebody he knew real well
but still couldn't quite figure out but couldn't stop thinking about,
either, and after awhile I just wanted to leave and go on to my other
classes, but once he got talking, Mr. Wells wouldn't shut up and he
got so close to me I could see the cigarette stains on his teeth. It felt
like being trapped on those deer platforms with my dad. Mr. Wells
shook his head and that was the first time I heard him talk about
the chaos theory and how it was revolutionizing the field of geol-
ogy, and he said, "Look here, in old days they thought every river
was evolving to a perfect state, to God's vision of what a river ought
to be, like the Shenandoah River, which is famous for its repeat-
ing bends like the letter *S* copying itself over and over, like some
snakes when they move, or like sound waves." Mr. Wells used the
word *sublime* in there somewhere, but he rolled his eyes when
he said it. He lit another cigarette and I thought of him looking
down on his mountain creek from one of his Colorado trees with
his graph paper and his compass and his instruments for taking
measurements of sines and cosines, and I asked him if everything
affected everything, how did he know when he was finished with
his research, and how could they give him a grade, and for that
matter what good was it all? He said, "Process. It's process," which
made no sense to me—none—and I avoided him as much as I
could after that.

6. Kerry Boss was hassling me about something not too long ago, telling me he was going somewhere with his dad, like to a football game, and he wouldn't shut up about it, about him and his dad, him and his dad, going to the game, got seats on the forty-yard line, lower level, and I finally said, "Shut up, Mister String-Around-Your-Dick. My dad used to take me hunting, and when I turn thirteen my mom's giving me his gun." When I got that gun, I told Kerry, I would probably kill him.

The day I rode my bike out to Montford Metals to see the wreck of my dad's truck, I stood on the hood of another old car, and looking down from there some things did finally add up: the angle, how fast, the nature of the impact. I was scientific about it that time, and even managed to look inside the cab, which I hadn't ever before. One of my X-Men comic books was there as if I'd just left it on the passenger seat and I thought it might be kind of a miracle, like a Bible being the only thing left after a church fire, but when I reached in to pick it up it was soggy and came apart in my fingers. After that I threw rocks for a while to try to bust the driver's side mirror, which had only gotten cracked a little from the wreck, but it wasn't too long before Mr. Montford came out and chased me off.

Afterward I started thinking maybe that was the one thing I learned from all of this—the one thing about human kindness. It isn't your mom telling you to talk to Reverend Mann when you're pretty sad, or Reverend Mann telling you everything's for a reason. It isn't that at all. It's a guy like Junior Delillo not being too disgusted with you for beating up a retarded kid that he won't pull Stevie Espenship off of you when things get turned around, or it's an old guy like Mr. Montford giving you a head start because he knows that's your dad's truck, giving you a chance to get away before he lets out his dogs and sics them on you in the junkyard.

My mom would think that's a hard way to look at things, and she'd probably say that about Mr. Wells and the chaos theory too. Her and Reverend Mann—I guess they do believe in a perfect river, but I'm not so sure myself. One of these days I'd like to go to Colorado to see Mr. Wells's little creek, and then go to the Shenandoah Valley to see that big, blue, winding river they've got over there, too. It's the kind of thing—maybe me and my dad would have gotten around to talking about it one day on the deer stand if the subject came up before he got too deep into his beers. It's the kind of thing—I think it must be hard all your life, and hard figuring out on your own.

# About the Author

STEVE WATKINS is the author of *The Black O: Racism and Redemption in an American Corporate Empire*, a nonfiction account of the largest employment discrimination class action lawsuit in U.S. history. He teaches Ashtanga yoga and works as an investigator and advocate for abused and neglected children through CASA, a child advocacy organization. For the past sixteen years, Watkins has also taught journalism, creative writing, and Vietnam War literature at the University of Mary Washington in Fredericksburg, Virginia, where he lives with his wife and four daughters.